GETTING EVEN

A CHARLOTTE ZOLOTOW BOOK

GETTING EVEN

MIRIAM CHAIKIN

DRAWINGS BY RICHARD EGIELSKI

1 8 📖 1 7

———— HARPER & ROW, PUBLISHERS ————

Cambridge, Philadelphia, San Francisco, London, Mexico City, São Paulo, Sydney

———— NEW YORK ————

In Memory of Ellen Brooke

Getting Even

Text copyright © 1982 by Miriam Chaikin
Illustrations copyright © 1982 by Richard Egielski

Library of Congress Cataloging in Publication Data
Chaikin, Miriam.
  Getting even.

  Summary: Molly, a young Jewish girl growing up in the Brooklyn of the 1940's, explores the power of friendship and jealousy.
  [1. Friendship—Fiction. 2. Jealousy—Fiction. 3. Jews—United States—Fiction] I. Egielski, Richard, ill. II. Title.
PZ7.C3487Ge 1982   [Fic]   81-48647
ISBN 0-06-021164-4   AACR2
ISBN 0-06-021165-2 (lib. bdg.)

First Edition

CHAPTER ONE

Tsippi's Secret

Molly lay in bed, under the covers where it was warm, waiting for Rebecca, her little sister, to leave the room they shared. Molly could not get dressed until Rebecca left. She needed privacy today.

Rebecca was not one to be rushed. She sat on the floor lacing up her shoes, grunting with each pull.

"Come on," Molly said, getting impatient. "Shake a leg. I have to get dressed for school."

Rebecca looked up. "So who's stopping you?"

"You're very fresh since you started kindergarten, you know that?" Molly said.

Rebecca shrugged. "I can't help it." She gave a final grunt, tied a bow, and was finished. Rising, she straightened her side of the bed—the side Molly wasn't in—and went from the room.

At last Molly was alone. She hurried out of bed and shut the door. In the privacy she had been waiting for, she opened her bureau drawer and took out a blue satin chemise, a hand-me-down from her rich cousins who lived near the park. When Molly first saw it, she had no idea what it was. Neither did Mama. Then Helen Baumfeld, the girl who lived upstairs, saw it hanging on the line and told Molly it was a chemise, a kind of fancy underwear that the women wore in France.

Molly put on the chemise and looked at herself in the mirror. The long winter was getting her down. She had been needing something to think about. Now she had it. Today was her gym day. And last night, before falling asleep, she had remembered the chemise. She could almost see the look of surprise on the faces of the girls in the locker room when they saw her wearing the chemise.

Suddenly, Rebecca opened the door. She was dressed in a snowsuit. "I'm ready," she said, waving her schoolbag, a tin box with a handle in which she kept Ruthie, her dented plastic doll, and some crayons.

Molly resented the intrusion. She grabbed her pajamas and covered herself. "Get out of here!" she yelled. The girls in school were one thing, but she didn't want her little sister seeing her in a chemise.

Rebecca glared at her. "She's crazy," she said, and left.

Molly again shut the door and returned to the sight of the icy-blue loveliness in the mirror. She didn't care if the room was cold and she was shivering. And she didn't care if only grown ladies wore chemises and if the underwear was too big for her. She loved the sky-blue satiny look and feel of it. She wondered, as she studied herself in the mirror, when she would start to develop. Tsippi, her best friend, had started. So had Big Naomi, a girl in their class. Nice Beverly, who was not in their class, already wore a brassiere.

Pulling the chemise away from her chest, Molly looked down. Nothing there. Flat.

"Molly!" Mama called from the kitchen. "Tsippi's here."

Molly gave herself a final glance in the mirror, then hurried to get dressed. Tsippi lived almost a block away, across from the school. Yet almost each morning she walked the extra block to Molly's house, just so they could walk to school together. Molly straightened her side of the bed and walked through the living room into the kitchen.

The radio, on the kitchen table, was on, and Mama sat holding the wire in back so the sound would come up. She was listening to the news. These days she was always listening to the news. Everyone was. Ever since Japan had bombed Pearl Harbor in December and President Roosevelt had declared war on Japan the next day.

Yaaki, Molly's little two-and-a-half-year-old brother, sat rolling a paper ball along the tabletop, humming to himself.

Molly noticed that Rebecca was in the foyer, waiting near the door. But where was Tsippi?

"I thought you said Tsippi was here," she said.

"She's in the bathroom," Rebecca said, nodding at a door near where she stood.

Molly went up to the table and took a sip from the cup of cocoa Mama had poured for her. Papa and Joey, her older brother, had eaten breakfast and left. They were the first ones out, Papa going to the haberdashery store where he worked and Joey off to Montauk, the junior high school two blocks away. Molly shoved aside the cups and plates they had left, clearing a space for herself, and stood buttering a roll.

Mama turned off the radio and stared at her. "That's how you eat, standing up like a horse?" she asked.

"I'm in a hurry," Molly said, biting into the roll.

"How long does it take to sit down?" Mama said.

Tsippi came strolling into the kitchen in her coat, muffler, and woolen hat. "Hi, Molly," she said. Her eyeglasses lacked an earpiece and hung down on one side. They had been broken for some time.

Molly noticed, as she hurried to finish eating, that Mama was looking Tsippi over. Molly knew what to expect.

"That's how a person should dress in winter," Mama said. "Not like you."

"Tsippi wouldn't wear all those clothes either if her stepmother didn't make her," Molly said. "Right, Tsippi?" she asked, turning to her friend.

Tsippi shrugged and nodded.

Mama removed some dishes from the table and brought them to the sink. "Don't come crying to me that your knees are bleeding from the cold," she said with a glance at Molly's bare knees.

Molly hated winter and hated being cold, but she refused to wear the heavy stockings and other old-lady winter clothes that Rebecca still wore. Molly gulped down her cocoa and wiped her mouth.

Yaaki began to hum in a loud voice, kicking his feet under the table to keep time. He looked so cute, with his golden curls and light-blue eyes, Molly couldn't resist him, and she bent and kissed his cheek. He pushed her away and continued his song.

"I'm ready," Molly said, going to the closet for her coat.

She put a hand in her coat pocket and drew out a nickel.

"Carfare for Sunday," she said, holding it up. She, Tsippi, and Little Naomi were planning to visit Jeanette and Estelle, two sisters who used to live in the neighborhood. Molly hardly remembered them, but it meant a

trolley ride to Church Avenue and she was always ready for a trip.

"My stepmother won t let me go," Tsippi said.

Molly looked at her friend with surprise. "Why not? She gave you permission already."

"She changed her mind," Tsippi said. "I'll tell you later," she whispered.

"You can't go either," Mama called from the sink.

"Why not?" Molly asked.

"It's Purim," Mama said.

Molly made a face. She had forgotten.

"Molly," Yaaki called. "I want paper."

Molly hurried to tear a used sheet from her notebook. Yaaki had tantrums. He looked like an angel, and acted like one, but if he got angry or something scared him he started screaming. Everyone gave in to him quickly, to avoid it.

Molly crumpled the sheet into a ball and gave it to him. She stood smiling down at him as he held it, watching the paper unroll, fascinated by the sound it made.

A grunt came from near the door. Molly knew without looking that Rebecca was shaking her knees with impatience.

Tsippi took Molly by the arm. "Let's go. I have to go to the bathroom," she said in a whisper.

Molly looked at her. "Didn't you just go?"

"I have to go again," Tsippi said.

"Then go," Molly said, nodding at the bathroom door. "I'll wait."

Tsippi shook her head. "I want to wait till I get to school. I'll tell you later," she added softly.

Molly wondered, as she opened the door, why Tsippi

was behaving so peculiarly and what secret she had to tell. It was gray and cold out. The snow had been cleared away from in front of the houses and piled up in dirty mounds along the curb. Molly tried not to speak when it was cold, believing she was warmer that way.

On the stoop, as Rebecca looked away, Molly glanced at Tsippi, expecting her friend to offer a hint with her mouth, but Tsippi only nodded at Rebecca, indicating she couldn't yet speak.

Molly squeezed her lips together, hunched up her shoulders against the cold, and took Rebecca by the hand.

"Be careful," she said, opening the side of her mouth, and led her sister down the steps.

Sometimes Molly was able to communicate with Tsippi mentally. She tried it now, concentrating hard to pick up Tsippi's thoughts, but she received no message.

The light was red at the corner and the girls stopped, waiting for it to change.

"Tsippi," Rebecca said, "when are you going to tell Molly?"

"Tell her what?" Tsippi asked.

"What you didn't tell her before."

Tsippi looked innocent. "I forgot what it was," she said, and gave Molly a wink when Rebecca turned away.

At the light change, Molly, Tsippi, and Rebecca hurried across and on into the school yard. They shuddered with relief as they entered the small hallway, where a radiator at the foot of the Up staircase hissed out warmth. Molly unsnapped her sister's hood and started the zipper down. The kindergarten was behind the stairs. Rebecca could manage the rest herself, when she got there.

"So long," Rebecca called, waving her tin box and disappearing around the stairs.

Molly turned to Tsippi eagerly. "Well?"

Tsippi began to blush. "Now I'm ashamed to tell you," she said.

"Why?" Molly asked, exasperated. "Don't I tell you everything?" She felt like a liar as soon as the words were out. She told Tsippi a lot, but not *everything*.

Molly and Tsippi stepped out of the way as the door opened to let in some kids. Ruthie Riness, a new girl in class, was among them.

"Hi," she said with a smile, stopping to speak. "It's my birthday in two Sundays," she said. "My parents are taking me to a restaurant. They said I could bring two friends. Can you come?"

Molly and Tsippi exchanged glances. They found Ruthie too friendly and thought she was trying too hard to get on the good side of people. The only good thing they could say about her was that her part was always straight.

"I'm not allowed to eat in restaurants—my family's kosher," Molly said, glad for the excuse.

"I have to ask my stepmother," Tsippi said.

Ruthie started up the stairs. "Let me know," she called.

Molly quickly turned back to Tsippi. "So?"

"I—my—I have . . ." Tsippi began.

Curious, Molly waited for her friend to continue.

"I'm—sick," Tsippi said, and began to giggle.

Molly felt cheated. She could not understand why Tsippi had carried on so if that was all it was. What kind of secret was that?

"Well, then why did your stepmother let you come to school, if you're sick?" she said, irritated.

"Not that kind of sick," Tsippi said. "Unwell. I got—*it*."

Molly stared at her friend in disbelief.

"You know, the period . . ." Tsippi said, explaining.

Molly knew older girls got a period once a month. But Tsippi was only eleven, a few months older than she.

"Remember, we heard the big girls talking about it that day?" Tsippi said. "The curse. The monthlies. The period. *It*."

Molly nodded. She knew what Tsippi was talking about. She just couldn't believe that Tsippi was talking about herself. She remembered hearing the girls talk that day. She had pretended to understand, but she hadn't; not really.

Tsippi reached into her schoolbag and took out a pamphlet. "My stepmother gave me this," she said. "It tells all about the period. It's called *Marjorie May's Twelfth Birthday*. You can keep it."

"But you're not twelve," Molly said.

"The book says you don't have to be," Tsippi said. "You can be any age."

"Then why do they say twelve?" Molly asked.

Tsippi shrugged.

Molly glanced at the pamphlet. She had better read it. That was the only way for her to find out about the period. She would not be hearing about it at home. Mama would never tell her. She would not be able to bring herself to speak of such things. Molly put the pamphlet in her schoolbag. As soon as she had some privacy, she would read it.

The door opened again and Rotten Beverly and Little Naomi came in. Little Naomi was not in Molly's class. But Rotten Beverly was. She was Molly's seatmate, and Molly couldn't stand her. "Hi, Naomi," Molly said, ignoring Beverly. "Tsippi can't go Sunday, and neither can I."

"I can't either," Little Naomi called from the stairs. "Company's coming."

"Hi, Tsippi," Beverly called, pointedly ignoring Molly and following Little Naomi up the stairs.

Tsippi turned to Molly. "We better go too," she said. "I have to go to the bathroom."

Molly had forgotten. She wondered, as she started up the stairs beside Tsippi, if the period made girls go to the bathroom more, and if it was all right for them to climb stairs. Her father had a weak heart. He couldn't climb stairs.

"Are you allowed to go up stairs?" She turned to Tsippi, beside her.

"According to my stepmother, I can't do anything for a week," Tsippi said. "But she's wrong. The book says it lasts about five days. And you can do everything, except maybe go horseback riding."

The girls laughed. Horseback riding was a sport for the rich and not something they had to worry about.

As they arrived at the third floor they saw Miss Tuck, arms folded, standing in front of their room, 323, and watching the hall.

Tsippi took Molly's arm and pulled her to a stop. "I

want to ask you something, Molly, but promise to tell me the truth," Tsippi said.

"I promise," Molly said, wondering what was coming now.

"Do I look different to you?" Tsippi asked.

"No, why?" Molly asked, looking her friend over.

"The book says I'm a woman now," Tsippi said, and paused. "Molly, I don't feel like a woman," she added.

"Good morning, girls," Miss Tuck called.

"Good morning, Miss Tuck," the girls answered.

The girls' bathroom was opposite room 323. Tsippi headed one way and Molly the other. Her head full of what she had just heard, she smiled up at Miss Tuck as she went in.

CHAPTER TWO

No Gym

As usual, Molly ignored Beverly and sat down. Her thoughts were on Tsippi. Her friend was blackboard monitor this week, and she watched as Tsippi went carefully over the board with the eraser, wiping it clean. Hard as Molly looked, she could see no difference in her friend.

"So what if she has the period and I don't?" Molly said to herself.

At the sound of the bell, Miss Tuck closed the door and went to her seat.

"Let's begin, class," she said.

The first subject was geography, and as Molly reached into her schoolbag for the book, the program changed.

"But not with geography," Miss Tuck added. "The products we import from Latin America can wait. It's a gloomy day, and I think we should cheer ourselves up. Let's find something appropriate in our readers."

Tickled with the surprise, Molly glanced over her shoulder at Tsippi to share the pleasure with her friend, and Tsippi smiled back. Molly drew out her reader instead, hoping the principal never found out what a good teacher Miss Tuck was. The teacher spoke very softly and Molly leaned forward to listen.

"Cheerful," Miss Tuck continued. "That will be our

theme. That means the following subjects are banned: winter, frost, cold, snow, war, heartbreak, and disappointment. Is that clear, class?"

"Yes, Miss Tuck," Molly answered with the others.

"Who will start?" the teacher asked.

Molly smiled to herself, enjoying the class. She loved Miss Tuck for hating the winter as much as she did and for never calling on anyone by surprise, and always asking for volunteers.

"Raymond," Miss Tuck called.

Raymond walked to the front of the room and read from the reader, a story about a boy with a faithful dog. Raymond was the handsomest boy in class, and he had a beauty mark under his left eye. As Molly listened to him read, she watched the beauty mark move.

"Any other volunteers?" Miss Tuck asked when Raymond was through.

"Miss Tuck, you read to us!" one of the boys called from the back.

"I'd rather listen to you today," the teacher said.

Molly flipped through the pages of her reader looking for a cheerful story.

"It need not be a story we know," Miss Tuck said. "You may tell about something interesting that happened to you, an amusing experience, anything—so long as it's cheerful."

The only thing of interest that Molly could think of was what Tsippi had told her. But that was Tsippi's experience, not hers. Besides, it wasn't cheerful.

"Spring, the beach, birds," Miss Tuck said, offering suggestions. "An anecdote, a poem . . ."

Molly perked up. She liked to write poems. She searched her mind for a starting line. "Bird . . . chird . . . fird . . ." she repeated to herself.

"Tsippi," Miss Tuck called.

Molly swung around in her seat to listen to Tsippi.

"It isn't a poem or anything, Miss Tuck," Tsippi said, straightening her eyeglasses. "You said birds. Tsippi, my name, is short for Tsipporah. It means bird in Hebrew."

Tsippi sat down abruptly, as if she were suddenly embarrassed, and Molly wondered if it was because of the period, or because in speaking her real name she was reminded of her real mother, who was dead.

"Thank you for telling us," Miss Tuck said. "Anyone else?"

Molly continued searching her mind for a rhyme. "Word . . . third . . . hird . . ."

"Angelina!" Miss Tuck called.

"Can it be a song?" Angelina asked.

"If it meets the requirements, yes," Miss Tuck said.

"It's about a bird," Angelina said.

"Come and sing it for us," Miss Tuck said.

"Hurray!" someone yelled from the back. Molly was excited too. She loved listening to Angelina sing. Mama and Joey had good voices, but Angelina had the best voice in the whole school.

Angelina went to the front and, facing the class, began to sing:

> "On a tree by the river a little tomtit
> Sang 'Willow, titwillow, titwillow!'
> And I said to him, 'Dickie-bird, why do you sit
> Singing "Willow, titwillow, titwillow?"

" 'Is it weakness of intellect, birdie,' I cried,
'Or a rather tough worm in your little inside?'
With a shake of his poor little head he replied,
'Oh, willow, titwillow, titwillow.' "

Molly clapped as hard as anyone when Angelina was
through. Suddenly the door opened and a messenger
came in with a note from the principal. Molly held her
breath. Notes from the principal always worried her. Papa
had a weak heart, Yaaki had tantrums, Mama had high
blood pressure. A note could be for her, telling her to
come home. Or it could be that the principal had found
out what a good teacher Miss Tuck was and was firing
her.

After reading the note, Miss Tuck looked up. "Mrs.
Rice, the girls' gym teacher, has gone home sick," she
said. "The boys will have gym as usual," she added.
"Girls, your makeup gym class will be on Wednesday."

Molly had forgotten about her chemise in the excitement of the morning. She had been looking forward to
showing it off.

"Girls, you have a choice," Miss Tuck said. "You can
use this period for recreation and go outside to play, if
it's not too cold for you, or you can stay here and read,
or do schoolwork. But there'll be no talking for those
who stay."

When the bell rang, the boys ran out. So did Providence
Lagezzi and some of the other "giants," as Molly and
Tsippi called the big girls in who sat in the rear of the
room.

Molly wouldn't have dreamed of going out into the
cold. She turned to Tsippi with a smile, knowing they

would both choose to stay inside, where it was warm; but she did not catch Tsippi's eye. Tsippi was leaning across the aisle, talking and laughing with Big Naomi.

The sight disturbed Molly, but she put it out of her mind. She decided to read the booklet Tsippi had given her. This was a good time. She never had any privacy at home. Her only concern was Beverly. Molly didn't want her seatmate to see what she was reading. Beverly liked sports, and Molly thought for a moment that she was going outside to play. But Beverly only fidgeted for a moment, then stayed put. She kept her reader open on the desk, as if she were reading, but under the desk, in her lap, she was adding rubber bands to her rubber-band ball.

Molly slipped the pamphlet out of her schoolbag and hid it in her reader. She slid to the opposite end of the seat, to get as far away from Beverly as possible, and, turning her back to Beverly, began to read.

A moment later Beverly nearly knocked her over, trying to get close enough to see what she was reading. Molly jerked the reader closed and stuck out her finger.

"See this finger?" she said as a warning.

Beverly knew what followed: *See this thumb? See this fist? Better run!* She never batted an eyelash. She only smiled and looked away.

Molly opened her book and tried again, but Beverly's breath was hot on her neck.

"Get away from me!" Molly said, annoyed.

"Miss Tuck!" Beverly sang out. "Molly's reading a dirty book."

Molly's anger flared as she heard gasps around the room. "I am not," she cried.

"There are naked people in it," Beverly said.

Molly felt herself redden, glad that there were no boys in the room.

Miss Tuck came marching over. "What are you reading, Beverly?" she asked.

Beverly hid the rubber-band ball in the folds of her skirt. "This story," she said, jabbing the page.

"What's the name of it?" Miss Tuck asked.

Beverly turned a few pages until she came to the name of the story. "Martha at the Farm," she said.

"Continue reading," Miss Tuck said. She turned to Molly. "May I see what you're reading, Molly?" she said.

Molly handed her the book, which fell open at the pamphlet. Miss Tuck looked it over, then turned to the class.

"It is not a dirty book," she said. "There are no naked people in it. It's a book of instruction, and the drawings are of parts of the body." She closed the pamphlet and gave it back to Molly.

"It meets the requirements of the day's theme," Miss Tuck continued, "and Molly has every right to be reading it."

She gave Molly the reader and returned to her desk.

Molly was so grateful to the teacher, she could have cried. She gave Beverly a look of disgust, then put the pamphlet away and took out her notebook. She was too upset to do anything but doodle, and as she sat making squares and circles a note was dropped on her desk.

Molly looked up and saw Ruthie Riness heading for the door. Molly opened the note and read it. *I knew Beverly was lying,* the note said.

Molly appreciated receiving the note. She watched for Ruthie to return and smiled at her as she took her seat. Molly's glance fell on Miss Tuck. She gave the teacher an embarrassed smile and returned to the sheet on her desk.

Dipping her pen into the inkwell for a fresh supply of ink, Molly wrote in her best hand and with great care: *I love Miss Tuck.* She looked at what she had written and felt that her handwriting had never been so clear, balanced, and lovely before. She sat admiring it for a while, then crossed the words out with heavy strokes so Beverly could not see what she had written.

Soon the lunch bell rang. Molly got her coat from the wardrobe and, as she did every day, went out into the hall to wait for Tsippi so they could walk out together. Her classmates came filing out. Molly smiled at Ruthie Riness as she walked by. Tsippi came walking out with Big Naomi.

"What happened?" Tsippi asked, rushing over.

"Yeah, what?" Big Naomi asked.

Molly did not especially want to speak in front of Big Naomi, but she had no choice.

"I was reading—that booklet you gave me," she said, heading for the stairs.

"I gave her *Marjorie May's Twelfth Birthday*," Tsippi explained to Naomi.

"Oh," Naomi said.

"That's what she called dirty?" Tsippi said.

"The pictures, you know . . ." Molly said.

"You mean the legs and the positions and that?" Tsippi said.

Molly nodded. "She was just trying to get me in Dutch. Miss Tuck knew that."

Molly took hold of the banister as she went down and squeezed it. "Oooo! The creep!" she said.

On the main floor, Tsippi turned to Molly. "Naomi has nobody to eat with. Her father's not home . . ." she began.

Naomi interrupted. "I have a sandwich. But I didn't want to eat alone. I asked Tsippi if I could eat with her. She eats alone too."

Molly felt funny, but she nodded. Tsippi ate lunch alone every day. Her stepmother and father both worked. Molly wondered why Naomi had to eat with Tsippi today. She watched the girls go, then went around the stairs to get Rebecca.

Rebecca was waiting for her in the hall. "I got a gold star today," Rebecca said.

"For what?" Molly asked, zipping up her sister's snowsuit.

"Courtesy," Rebecca answered, looking pleased.

Molly didn't think that was anything to brag about, but she said nothing.

"Where's Tsippi?" Rebecca asked.

"She had to go home," Molly said, wondering again why Big Naomi and Tsippi had to be eating together. She took her sister's hand and led her outside. *So what if Big Naomi has the period too?* she said to herself, hurrying to get home.

As she drew near the house she could see a large wooden object lying on the curb, in front of the house.

"What's that?" Rebecca asked.

Molly wasn't sure. They hurried over for a closer look.

"It's an icebox," Rebecca said. "Is it ours?"

Molly wondered. "Let's go see," she said from a crack at the side of her mouth, and ran up the steps.

CHAPTER THREE

Surprises

Molly and Rebecca stood in the kitchen looking from a huge, shiny, gleaming, new, white refrigerator against the wall to the table, where Mama, Papa, and Bessie, Papa's sister, sat drinking coffee. Molly had wondered, when she first saw them, what her father was doing at home in the middle of the day and why her aunt, who visited only on weekends, was there. But the white giant in the kitchen had stolen her breath—and her questions.

"*Nu*," Mama said, "what do you think of the surprise?"

"Some surprise," Molly said, filled with wonder. She turned to Mama. "Why didn't you tell us this morning?" she asked.

"What kind of surprise would it be if I told you?" Mama answered.

Yaaki was sitting on the floor in a metal basin. It was his own private place and he moved it from room to room. He got out of it and put his ear to the refrigerator. "Listen to it," he said. He liked sounds more than any toy, and he stood listening, with a look of enjoyment on his face.

Molly and Rebecca put their ears to the refrigerator and heard a soft hum. Molly opened the door and looked inside. "How clean and neat, Ma," she said. "And look, you don't have to bend down to reach the bottom."

Mama grinned from ear to ear. "And I don't have to

buy ice, or mop up the wet from the dripping," she said.

"Wait till Joey sees it," Molly said, thinking of her older brother and imagining the look of surprise on his face when he came home from school.

"Children, take off the coats," Mama said.

Molly and Rebecca hung up their coats in the closet and sat down at the table with the others. Everyone sat facing the refrigerator, admiring it.

"Ma," Rebecca said. "Are we rich?"

Mama laughed.

"We're not rich," Papa said. "Mama paid for it a dollar a week."

"I bought it eighteen months ago," Mama said. "It's a good thing too," she added. "Now, since the war started, everything goes to make guns and bullets for the soldiers. You can't buy a refrigerator today for love of money."

"Love *or* money, Ma," Molly said, correcting her mother. She wondered, after she had said it, if that was right. Suddenly *or* didn't sound right to her either.

"Well, the kids are home, so what are we waiting for?" Papa said.

Mama clapped a hand to her face. "Oy! Look at me! I forgot!" she said. She went to the refrigerator, took out the tuna fish sandwiches, and brought them to the table, along with a dish of gherkins.

Molly helped herself to a sandwich. She felt happy and watched idly as Mama cut up a sandwich for Yaaki and gave it to him on a plate.

"There's another surprise," Papa said.

Molly realized she had forgotten to find out. "Hey, how come you're not working, Pa?" she asked.

"That's the second surprise," he said. "I quit my job." He nodded at Bessie, across the table. "My sister got me a job in her place," he added, looking pleased.

Molly's heart leaped with joy. "A defense job?" she asked.

Papa nodded.

Molly knew from hearing her parents speak that a defense job was the best job a person could have. It meant steady work and good pay. She felt a shudder of delight. Papa could stop worrying about losing his job now.

"Are we rich?" Rebecca asked again.

Papa laughed. "Richer than before, but not rich," he said.

Molly had never seen her parents looking so happy. It made her want to cry. She took a bite of sandwich to hide her face. "God bless America," she said to herself, on the point of tears.

Rebecca sat lifting the top piece of bread on each of the remaining sandwiches and looking inside. She accepted no tuna fish in her mayonnaise, and Mama had to make a special sandwich for her. "Ma, where is my sandwich?" she asked.

Mama got up from the table. "Excuse me," she said. "I forgot in the excitement." She removed a sandwich from the refrigerator and gave it to Rebecca.

Molly sat thinking about the news. "I don't like so many surprises in one day." She looked at Papa. "Why couldn't you get the new job next week, Pa, so we could have another surprise then?"

Papa smiled. "Life doesn't work that way," he said.

Bessie stirred her coffee with a spoon. "The boss got

a big order from the government," she said. "He needs workers now, not next week." She took a sip of coffee. "Ptu!" she said, making a face. "This is horseradish, not coffee."

Molly and the others around the table exchanged smiles. Bessie could be counted on to say that about the poor grade of coffee civilians had to drink since the war had started.

"The real coffee is for the soldiers," Rebecca said, repeating a phrase she had heard often.

Molly again wondered why her aunt was there. "How come you're not working?" she asked.

"The boss gave me off," Bessie said.

Molly had a feeling that that was not the whole truth. She suspected that Bessie's presence in Borough Park on a weekday had something to do with Bessie's husband, Heshy, whom Molly did not like. "Where's Heshy?" she asked.

"Working," Bessie said, and glanced at Mama.

Molly was even more suspicious now. Heshy was a waiter in Coney Island, at the beach. Last summer Molly had overheard her aunt complaining that Heshy was lazy, that he didn't like to work. She wondered how he could be working now, in the winter, when no one went to Coney Island.

Bessie took another sip. "Ptu!" she said again.

"Don't finish," Mama said. "I'll bring tea."

She got up and brought glasses to the table, and poured tea for Papa, Bessie, and herself. Bessie took a lump of sugar from her pocketbook and broke it in three. She gave Mama and Papa each a piece. They put the sugar between their teeth and sipped tea through it.

Molly wished her parents and aunt were more modern. "When are you going to drink tea like Americans, with the sugar inside?" she said.

"It tastes better this way," Bessie said. She took the empty plate that Yaaki held up to her and put it in the sink behind her.

Molly spotted Bessie's suitcase in the living room, under the picture of Jabotinsky, the Jewish leader. "Are you sleeping over?" she asked excitedly.

Bessie nodded. "And I don't want any snoring from you or Rebecca," she said with a straight face after a moment.

Molly knew her aunt liked to kid around and she played along.

"Snoring!" she said. "I don't snore, and neither does Rebecca."

"Somebody snores," Bessie said, looking innocent.

"It's you," Rebecca said, smiling.

"Me?" Bessie asked.

The look of surprise on her face made Molly and Rebecca laugh. Bessie used to kid around all the time, before she got married, and Molly had almost forgotten how much fun her aunt could be.

"We learned a new song in school today," Rebecca said. "Want to hear it?"

Molly winced. Rebecca's singing voice was almost as bad as her own. "Wait till Joey comes home," she said, hoping to sneak away before then.

"I'll sing it for him again," Rebecca said.

"Sing it," Yaaki said from the basin.

Molly gave up. "Hurry up then," she said. "I have to go back to school."

Rebecca positioned herself in front of the refrigerator and, swinging her arms from side to side, like an elephant's trunk, sang,

> "The elephant carries a great big trunk—
> He never packs it with clothes.
> It has no lock and it has no key,
> But he takes it wherever he goes."

Molly remembered the song from when she was small and in kindergarten. She clapped along with the others.

"Laya!"

The voice came from the courtyard. It was Mrs. Baumfeld, calling Mama to the phone.

Mrs. Baumfeld lived upstairs. She was the only tenant in the building who had a telephone.

Mama opened the window.

"Close the window, I'm freezing," Rebecca said.

Molly hugged herself against the cold.

"It's your sister," Mrs. Baumfeld called. "She said it was nothing to worry about."

"I'll be right up," Mama said, and shut the window. "I wonder what Esther wants," she said, sounding worried and heading for the door.

"You heard Mrs. Baumfeld say it was nothing to worry about," Papa said.

As Mama left, Papa opened his paper and read it and Bessie brought milk and cookies to the table. Molly filled a glass with milk and took a cookie. A moment later the door opened and Joey came in. She watched him eagerly, waiting for him to see the refrigerator, but he never noticed. He took off his coat and sat down at the table.

"I'm hungry," he said, taking a sandwich from the plate.

Molly couldn't believe it. She saw Papa put down his paper, preparing to tell his news, but she signaled him to wait.

"Joey, didn't you see anything?" she asked.

Joey glanced around. "Where's Mama?"

"Not that," Molly said.

"It's cold in here. The landlord didn't give heat?"

"Not that either," Molly said. "Are you blind?" she asked, exasperated. "What's that on the wall next to the sink, where the icebox used to be?"

Joey turned to look. "A refrigerator!" he said.

"Didn't you see the old icebox outside?" Rebecca asked.

"I didn't know it was ours," he said. He glanced around the table. "No gherkins?" he asked, staring at the empty dish.

"I'll bring more," Bessie said, getting up from the table.

Molly didn't think her aunt ought to be waiting on her brother. "Why don't you let him get it himself?" she said.

"You're just jealous because I'm her favorite," Joey said.

Molly had suspected that that was true, but she didn't like to hear it.

"I have no favorites," Bessie said. "I love everyone the same."

"You should be ashamed of yourself," Molly said to her brother, "making an old lady wait on you."

"Who's an old lady?" Bessie asked.

· 27 ·

Molly looked up. She hadn't meant it to sound that way. "Excuse me, I didn't mean it," she said, embarrassed.

"Please," Papa said, opening his newspaper. "I'm getting a headache."

"Me too," Rebecca said, and put her fingers in her ears.

"Did you hear about Papa's new job?" Molly asked Joey.

"How could I? I just got home." He turned to Papa. "What new job?" he asked.

"A defense job, in Bessie's place," Papa said proudly.

"A defense job! Wow!" Joey said.

Molly could see the pride in her brother's face.

"I learned a new song in school, Joey," Rebecca said. "You want to hear it?"

"Sing it again," Yaaki said from the basin.

"We heard it already," Molly said.

"I asked Joey, not you," Rebecca said.

"Not now, I'm eating. Later, maybe," Joey said.

The door opened and Mama came flying in, grinning. "I'm fainting," she said.

Everyone jumped up from the table and spoke at once. "What happened?" "What is it?"

Molly saw a worried look cross Yaaki's face. If he got scared, it might bring on a fit. "Mama's smiling, Yaaki. See?" she said reassuringly.

"What happened?" Bessie repeated, trotting along beside Mama.

Mama dropped into a chair.

"What is it? Tell us," Papa said.

"You won't believe it," Mama said, still grinning.

"*Nu*, tell us already," Bessie said.

"My sister is getting married," Mama said.

Molly was shocked. "Esther?" she asked.

"So many years a widow, and now she's getting married," Mama said.

"Mazel tov!" "Congratulations!" Papa and Bessie called together.

"We'll have a new uncle," Joey said, helping himself to another sandwich.

Molly was embarrassed. She had heard some stories about what married people do. She didn't believe the stories. Even so, last year, when Bessie had gotten married, Molly had thought she was too old. Aunt Esther was even older.

"Mordi will have a stepfather now," she said, feeling she ought to say something. The word reminded her of Tsippi, the only other child she knew who had a stepparent.

"I can't believe it," Mama repeated softly, smiling to herself.

Molly noticed Bessie looking sad again. She remembered a conversation she had overheard.

"He's running around with a waitress from his place, a greenhorn," Bessie had said, speaking about her husband.

Mama had spat. *"Gobbich!"* she had answered. "Bums! Tramps! The both of them."

Now Molly went up to Bessie and put an arm around her.

Bessie smiled, showing a gold tooth. "So?" she said. "Is it okay if I share your room?"

"I like it when you're here," Molly answered. "It's more fun."

"It's my room, too," Rebecca said.

"Is it okay with you if I sleep in your room?" Bessie asked.

"I like it when you're here too," Rebecca said.

CHAPTER FOUR

Bessie Stays

Molly hurried to school to tell Tsippi the news. As she rushed down the hall she saw her friend up ahead.

"Tsippi!" she called.

Tsippi stopped and waited for Molly to catch up.

"Guess what," Molly said. "My father has a new job, and we have a new refrigerator!"

Molly could see her friend was impressed. Tsippi was one of the richest girls Molly knew. Her father had a job in the post office. He even had a car.

"Not only that," Molly continued. "My aunt Bessie is sleeping over tonight. I think she's going to start living with us again, the way she used to, before she got married." Molly thought about Aunt Esther's news but could not bring herself to mention it.

"Is she getting a divorce?" Tsippi asked.

"I don't know," Molly said. She didn't want to say more. The conversations she had overheard were private, and a family matter.

Big Naomi came walking up to them. She nodded toward the classroom. "You going in?" she asked.

Molly felt a flush of resentment and said nothing. She wondered what Tsippi and Big Naomi had discussed at lunch.

"In a minute," Tsippi said.

Ruthie Riness came out of the girls' room, across the hall, and started to join them.

"They're not going in yet," Big Naomi said, moving toward the classroom. Ruthie smiled at Molly and Tsippi and followed Big Naomi inside.

Molly was grateful that Tsippi got rid of Big Naomi. She took her friend's arm and squeezed it. "We better go too," she said.

The afternoon went quickly—math, then music, which Molly hated, because she couldn't carry a tune and the teacher made her sit in back, with the other listeners. After that she went back to Miss Tuck's room and before she knew it the three-o'clock bell was ringing. Molly got her coat from the wardrobe and went out into the hall to wait for Tsippi.

"Are you coming to my house to do homework?" Molly asked as they walked down the hall together.

"I can't," Tsippi said. "They're taking me to buy me new shoes, then to get new glasses." She grinned. "They started treating me like a princess since I got the period," she added.

Molly could not see the connection, but she smiled anyhow. She opened the door to the school yard and both of them went out.

"If I get finished early, I'll come," Tsippi said at the gate. She lived just opposite, in the apartment house across the street.

Molly hoped Tsippi would come, but it was too cold to speak so she hunched up her shoulders and went home.

Mama, Bessie, and Rebecca were in the living room, listening to a soap opera on the radio. Papa and Yaaki were in the kitchen. Yaaki filled his basin with newspaper and brought it into the living room. Molly sat down on the arm of the easy chair in the living room to hear the end of *Life Can Be Beautiful*, then took her books and went into Joey's room to do homework. She wondered, as she finished one subject and began another, if Tsippi would be coming over. Soon it became too noisy for her to think. She looked up. Mama, Bessie, and Rebecca were bustling around the kitchen. She couldn't see Yaaki, but she could hear him. He was sitting in his basin in the living room, blowing on the plastic flute Bessie had bought for him in the five-and-ten.

As Molly got up to close the door of Joey's room she saw Tsippi step into the kitchen from the outside. Tsippi's glasses now sat firmly on her nose.

"Look everyone, Tsippi has new glasses," Molly called.

They all came to see and stood admiring the glasses, which were just like the old ones except that they had two earpieces. Tsippi took off her coat. She went up to the refrigerator and touched it and clucked over it.

"Come on, Tsippi," Molly said. "I was doing homework in Joey's room. He's at the Democratic Club, lifting weights."

In Joey's room, behind the closed door, they sat with their legs up on the bed, facing the courtyard window. Molly was curious and tried to find out what she could about lunchtime.

"Did Big Naomi make her own sandwich?" she asked.

"Her father made it," Tsippi said. "Sometimes she goes to eat with him by the pushcart, if it's not too cold. Sometimes she goes to her uncle's store. Today both of them had to go someplace, and she had nobody to eat with."

"You eat alone every day," Molly said.

"I'm used to it," Tsippi said.

"Did you talk about—you know—the period?" Molly asked.

Tsippi nodded. "Some of the time," she said. "She knows all the girls in school who get it," she added with a smile.

Molly didn't like hearing that. She knew those girls stuck together. They called the other girls babies. She hoped Tsippi wasn't going to be like that.

"Are you going to Ruthie Riness's birthday?" she asked, changing the subject.

Tsippi shook her head. "I'm not even going to ask my stepmother. I don't want to go if you don't go."

Molly remembered the note Ruthie had dropped on her desk and told Tsippi about it.

"I wonder how she gets such a straight part in her hair" was all Tsippi said.

Molly shrugged.

"She's nice, but she smiles too much," Tsippi said.

Molly remembered that Ruthie was the newest girl in the class. She also remembered what it felt like to move to a new neighborhood. She had been miserable when her parents decided to move from the Lower East Side to Borough Park in Brooklyn. She had been lost without her old friends, and felt like a stranger.

"She's still new. She doesn't have any friends yet. Maybe that's why," she said.

Tsippi slid down off the bed. "I better go. I told my stepmother I would be home before supper," she said.

Molly went with Tsippi to the door.

"See you in the morning," she said.

"Maybe," Tsippi said, pointing to her stomach. "I almost didn't come today. I had cramps at first," she added in a whisper.

Molly wasn't sure, as she waved good-bye, that she was going to like having the period when it came.

Later, when Joey came home looking all pink and healthy from lifting weights, everyone sat down for supper. Most of the conversation was about Papa's new job, the new refrigerator, and Yaaki's flute. It had stopped playing. But he said that he didn't care and that he liked it better this way. For Molly, the nicest part of the evening was seeing Aunt Bessie moving about the house. It was cozy with her aunt there.

"The president is coming on soon," Papa said after supper. "Bring in the radio, Joey."

Joey brought the radio in from the living room and put it on the kitchen table and plugged it in.

Molly saw that this would be a good time to read Tsippi's pamphlet. With everyone in the kitchen, she would have the living room to herself.

"I'll be in later—I have to finish something for school first," she said, going into her room. She took the pamphlet from her schoolbag and sat down on the couch to read it. She could hear the president's voice, but her attention was on the words of the pamphlet. She could not get a clear understanding of the period. The pamphlet spoke more about tubes and eggs than about what happens to a girl.

When she was finished, she put the pamphlet away and went into the kitchen to join the family around the table.

The president spoke on.

"Here are three high purposes for every American," he said.

"One, we shall not stop work for a single day. If any dispute arises, we shall keep on working while the dispute is solved by mediation, or conciliation or arbitration—until the war is won.

"Two, we shall not demand special gains or privileges or special advantages for any one group or occupation.

"Three, we shall give up conveniences and modify the routine of our lives if our country asks us to do so. We will do it cheerfully, remembering that the common enemy seeks to destroy every home and every freedom in every part of our land."

When the president's speech was over, and the band played the national anthem, Papa shut the radio off.

Molly looked at her aunt across the table. "Did you hear what he said?" she asked.

"Sure I heard," Bessie said. "About what?" she asked.

"About giving things up cheerfully," Molly said.

Bessie put a hand over her heart. "And I don't?" she asked innocently. "I give up everything cheerfully."

"Coffee too?" Molly asked.

"Well, almost everything . . ." Bessie said.

Everyone laughed.

When it came time to go to sleep, Papa went to the closet and removed the folding bed that Bessie used to sleep on before she was married and set it up against the wall in Molly and Rebecca's room.

Bessie watched as he opened it.

"Remember, no snoring," she said to the girls.

Molly and Rebecca looked at each other and laughed.

CHAPTER FIVE

Gym

Wednesday morning—the makeup gym today. Molly again put on the chemise. She hurried to finish breakfast when Tsippi came to call for her. Mama stood over a bag of laundry, taking out items of clothing and folding them.

"Tsippi, you'll come to us on Sunday, yes?" Mama said.

"What's Sunday?" Tsippi asked.

"Purim," Mama said. Mama knew that Tsippi's parents were Communists and did not celebrate Jewish holidays, but that Tsippi loved them.

"Will I ever!" Tsippi said.

"Sure she's coming," Molly added, going to the closet for her coat. Rebecca was already dressed and at the door.

"You'll eat *hamantaschen* with us, then we'll go to the synagogue to hear them read the Story of Esther."

"Boy, I remember those *hamantaschen* from last year," Tsippi said, rolling her eyes and licking her lips.

Yaaki walked by and Tsippi bent to give him a hug. "*Ooo*," she said, squeezing him.

"My flute broke," he said, showing her the toy.

"Oh, too bad," Tsippi said.

"Will you bring me a present?" he asked.

"Sure," Tsippi said.

"Ma," Rebecca called from the door, "Yaaki's asking for a present."

Mama was putting the things that needed to be ironed aside, on a chair. "It's not so terrible when he asks for a present," she said. "A piece of paper doesn't cost much."

"Let's go," Molly said, buttoning her coat and opening the door.

Miss Tuck rolled the wall map down over the blackboard, then took her seat. She opened her newspaper and began to read the war news aloud. Molly leaned forward to listen, hearing names like Manila, Malaya, and other strange-sounding places she had never heard of before.

Miss Tuck went to the board, took the pointer from the shelf, and stood beside the map.

"Here, on the right, are the Philippine Islands," she said, pointing. "And here, on this side, is Europe." She went to the other side of the map. "This is England," (point) "France," (point) "and this orange shape over here" (point, point) "is Poland." She replaced the pointer and perched on the edge of her desk.

"War affects us all," she said. "The boys who are far away from home are fighting for freedom and risking their lives. We at home are affected to a much lesser degree."

She glanced around the room. "We merely face shortages and inconveniences," she said.

"This newspaper," she said, hefting it, "weighs much less than it used to. Each sheet is thinner, and there are fewer sheets. If any of you heard President Roosevelt last night, you will have some idea why."

Molly wondered why. She thought back to the evening

and concluded that she had missed that part of the president's speech while she was reading.

"Can anyone tell us why the newspaper is thinner?" Miss Tuck asked.

Molly smiled to herself as she watched Beverly raise her hand. Beverly fooled no one. The teacher, and everyone, knew her tricks. She half raised her hand and twiddled a finger, as if she had the answer, but if Miss Tuck called on her she would say her hand wasn't up.

"Bernie," Miss Tuck called.

Molly turned to listen.

"Paper comes from the wood of trees, and the government needs the wood to build barracks for the soldiers to live in."

Miss Tuck nodded.

"I forgot," Bernie said, bouncing up again. "We make cardboard out of wood, to send food, blankets, and other supplies to soldiers and sailors," he added.

"And marines!" someone called from the rear.

Miss Tuck walked to the window side of the room. "What other shortages are we experiencing? Anyone?" she asked.

"We can't have bright lights anymore," Raymond answered. "We have to obey the dimout order, and use smaller light bulbs, and keep the window shades down at night, so enemy planes and ships can't find Brooklyn."

"Miss Tuck!" The voice came from the rear, where the giants sat. Molly recognized it as Providence's.

"They make gas masks and parachutes out of silk and rubber, and now my mother and aunts can't get silk stockings or girdles anymore," she said.

Molly laughed along with the rest of the class. She

turned to share the joke with Tsippi, but Tsippi wasn't looking her way. She was looking at Big Naomi and they were laughing together. Her happy mood broken, Molly faced front again. She tried to push the worry away.

"That'll do, class," Miss Tuck said. "That's right, Providence," she continued. "American boys are risking their lives. The least we can do is give up a few things."

"Miss Tuck!" Beverly said. "Please call on me."

"Beverly!"

"You can't get chocolate anymore, either. It's for the soldiers," Beverly said.

Miss Tuck folded her arms and nodded. "The products that go into making chocolate are scarce—sugar, cacao beans. Coffee is scarce too."

Molly thought of the look on her aunt's face when she drank coffee and raised her hand. Miss Tuck nodded.

"My aunt loves coffee," Molly said, "but all she can get is the imitation coffee, and she hates it."

"Boo-hoo! Too bad!" a boy's voice called from the back.

Angry, Molly turned to the back. "My aunt is not complaining," she said, not knowing who had spoken. "She gives cheerfully," she added, remembering the president's words. "I was just giving Miss Tuck an example."

"Yes," Miss Tuck said, "the absence of coffee is felt by many people, myself included. The absence of chocolate, too," she added with a smile. Everyone knew how much Miss Tuck loved chocolate.

"Tsippi," Miss Tuck called.

Tsippi rose. "My father has a car," she said. "He can only get gasoline once in a while, because of the rationing.

They need the gasoline for the war, for planes and tanks."

Miss Tuck came away from the window and sat at her desk again. "Well, that is what life is like in wartime," she said. "We in this country are lucky. We only have to give up a few comforts. Our allies suffer deeply. The war is being fought on their land. England is bombed almost daily by German planes."

Molly shuddered. She had seen pictures of bombings in the newsreels, when she went to the movies. She had heard her mother and father speak of the thousands of Jews that Hitler was killing and wondered how God could let such an evil man like Hitler live.

The period bell rang and everyone got up. "Girls," Miss Tuck said, "don't forget that you have gym today."

Molly took up her schoolbag and went out into the hall to wait for Tsippi. She was surprised to see her friend come out carrying a coat. Big Naomi was with Tsippi. Molly felt funny, seeing them together again.

"So long," Big Naomi said, heading for the staircase and the gym.

Ruthie Riness sat in back and was among the last to leave class. "Hey, Naomi, wait for me," she called down the hall, and ran to catch up.

Jealous was what Molly supposed she was. Another time she might have discussed it with Tsippi, but not now. She didn't want to be thought of as babyish.

"How come you have your coat?" she asked.

"I'm not taking gym. I'm going home," Tsippi said. "My stepmother gave me a note on Monday. I still have it."

As they headed down the hall, Molly remembered with regret that she was wearing her chemise. Things had been different when she had first gotten the idea. Now, Tsippi was going home and Molly would have to face the girls in the locker room alone. She wished she were wearing regular underwear.

"You know my stepmother," Tsippi continued. "The book says you can do everything, but she doesn't want me to do anything. Not even brush my teeth."

Molly pretended to be amused and smiled thinly. She took hold of the banister and went down the stairs.

Mrs. Rice, in the gym, was wearing her green gym bloomers, and a whistle around her neck. Tsippi went up to the teacher and gave her the note.

"Okay, you're excused, Tsippi," Mrs. Rice said when she had read it.

Tsippi turned to go. "See you later," she called to Molly over her shoulder.

Feeling dejected, Molly walked to the locker room, wishing there were some way for her to get out of displaying the chemise. In the locker room Ruthie Riness, Big Naomi, and some other girls were standing around and measuring themselves to see who was tallest. Molly walked around them to get to her locker, against the wall. Beverly had a locker in the same row and was getting undressed.

Molly took out her gym suit. Papa had ironed it Sunday night and it looked crisp and clean, but she couldn't bring herself to take off her clothes and put it on. She did not want to be seen in her chemise now, especially not by Beverly. Yet she couldn't just stand there. Around her, everyone was changing into gym suits.

When Molly saw Beverly bend to tie her laces, she thought if she hurried she could undress and dress before

Beverly looked up. Quickly, she got out of her clothes.

"Look at that, a bathing suit in the middle of winter!" Beverly said in a loud voice.

What Molly had feared had happened. "It's not a bathing suit, smart aleck," she said.

All the girls in the row turned to look.

"What is it?" Angelina asked.

"Underwear," Molly said. "They call it a chemise."

"I know what it is," Providence said. "It's for summer. My mother wears it. BRR," she added, with a shiver, "it makes me freeze to look at her."

The more Molly hurried to get her foot through the leg hole, the more she kept missing it.

"It's for ladies, not young girls," another voice chimed in.

Molly felt red and shrunken with embarrassment. She was glad to see Ruthie Riness appear.

"It's satin. I think it's pretty," Ruthie said.

The girls ran out, laughing.

The room was cold and Molly hurried to finish changing; then she and Ruthie went into the gym. Big Naomi, Providence, and some others were clustered around Mrs. Rice.

"Okay, girls," Mrs. Rice said. "Basketball teams, go to the court and play. You other girls, line up with your seatmates from class. We're going to race." She blew into her whistle. *Peep!*

Molly was miserable. On top of everything else, now she had to run against Beverly. The one thing Beverly was good at was sports. Hating the idea of having to lose to her seatmate, Molly took her place in line beside Beverly.

Peep!

The first two girls ran off.

Molly watched with dread as each pair of girls ran off, making the line shorter and shorter and bringing her turn closer. Contrary to the way Molly felt, Beverly could hardly wait to run, and stood hopping and jumping in place. With a sinking heart Molly watched herself get closer to the front of the line.

Peep!

The two girls in front of her ran off.

"Molly and Beverly!" Mrs. Rice said.

Molly bent to touch the floor and get into position. Beside her, Beverly did the same.

"Get set!" Mrs. Rice said.

Peep!

Beverly sprang forward and began to run, but Molly couldn't budge. She felt nailed to the spot. Mrs. Rice came walking up to her.

"What happened?" she asked.

Molly couldn't say. "I didn't hear the whistle," she answered, feeling stupid.

"You didn't hear . . . ?" Mrs. Rice began. "Okay, never mind," she said. "I'll blow it louder. Let's start again. Beverly!" she called, motioning Beverly to come back.

Beverly gave Molly a dirty look as she returned to the line.

"Get ready!" Mrs. Rice called.

Both girls touched the ground.

"Get set!"

Peep!

Beverly was again off like a shot, but Molly ran along,

trailing behind her and not even trying. There was no point trying. Beverly was a fast runner. Molly couldn't have won even if she had started ahead. Beverly stood at the finish line, grinning.

Twerp! Jerk! Molly said to herself, hating the look of victory on Beverly's face.

Mrs. Rice organized other races, but Molly managed to stay out of them. Instead, she got a jump rope. And she and Ruthie played together and took turns jumping until one of them missed.

"Okay, girls, get dressed," Mrs. Rice said when the bell rang.

Molly was in no hurry to get to the locker room. She did not want to go through the same thing again. She walked slowly along, with Ruthie beside her.

"Tsippi said she can't come on my birthday," Ruthie said.

Molly felt sorry for Ruthie. "Her stepmother is strict," she said, to make Ruthie feel better.

"We beat the other team," Big Naomi called as she ran by.

"Great!" Ruthie answered.

Molly wanted to delay getting into the locker room. Her intention was to let everyone get dressed and get out, so she could change in private. She paused at the bathroom door. "I'll see you later," she said. "I have to go."

CHAPTER SIX

Rye Bread, Unsliced

When Molly got back to class for her coat, the wardrobe was empty and the kids were all gone, but Miss Tuck was still there, sitting at her desk and eating lunch. She looked up.

"Molly, would you bring me a candy bar on the way back?" she asked. "A Milky Way, if they have it," she added.

Molly found the teacher's friendliness healing. Miss Tuck had a sweet tooth and often asked Molly to stop at the candy store. Molly was happy to do it. She took the coin the teacher held out.

"They didn't have Milky Ways the last time," Molly said apologetically. Chocolate had become scarce since the war had started.

"I know," Miss Tuck said. "Whatever you get will be fine," she added with a smile.

Molly left the room and went downstairs to get her little sister. She found Rebecca waiting for her in the hall.

"Where were you?" Rebecca asked.

"What am I, your slave?" Molly said, zipping up Rebecca's hood and taking her by the hand.

Outside, as she hurried Rebecca through the school yard, rushing to get home and out of the cold, Molly couldn't stop thinking about her humiliation in the locker room, the girls' remarks about the chemise, their laughter, her own shame.

"That's what you get for showing off," she muttered to herself. "Serves you right. You deserved it. Let's hope you learned a lesson and never do it again."

Rebecca tripped and Molly grabbed her hand more tightly.

"Watch it," she said from the corner of her mouth.

"I am watching it. You're pulling me," Rebecca answered.

Molly returned to her dismal thoughts. "Crime doesn't pay," she said aloud and with fervor, forgetting herself and not realizing that her voice was carrying, "and neither does showing off."

"What did I do?" Rebecca asked.

"Nothing. Why?" Molly asked, speaking again from the slit in her mouth.

"You said crime doesn't pay."

"I was talking to myself," Molly said.

"Then how come I heard?"

"Don't you ever talk to yourself?"

"Nobody can hear me when I talk to myself," Rebecca said.

The light was with them and Molly hurried Rebecca across the street.

"I'm going to tell Mama," Rebecca said.

"Tell her what?" Molly asked out of the corner of her mouth.

"You said I stole something."

Molly dropped her sister's hand. "Are you crazy?" she said, too irritated to be cautious and speaking normally. "When did I say that?"

"You said crime doesn't pay," Rebecca said.

"I told you, I was talking to myself," Molly repeated.

"Then how come I heard?" Rebecca asked again.

Molly couldn't stand it. Rebecca was driving her nuts. There was only one way to silence her little sister.

"I apologize," Molly said, trying to hide the irritation in her voice. "I didn't mean it. I promise never, ever to do it again, as long as I live."

Rebecca looked at her, then glanced away and walked home alone.

Not caring for any part of this day, Molly sulked, following behind.

After lunch Molly stopped at the candy store and bought Miss Tuck a Mary Jane. There was very little to choose from and it was the best candy bar she could find.

"No Milky Way?" Miss Tuck asked when Molly gave it to her.

Molly felt guilty, as if it were her fault. "Nothing with chocolate," she said.

"Never mind," Miss Tuck said. "Thanks," she added with a smile as she unwrapped a piece and put it in her mouth.

Molly waved to Tsippi as she hung up her coat and, when the starting bell rang a moment later, motioned to her friend that she would wait for her in the hall. Assembly was the first class after lunch, and the girls went down to the auditorium together. It was for the whole sixth grade, and they saw Little Naomi, Nice Beverly, and Julie there and waved to them. For a change, assembly was enjoyable, with an all-girl band from a school in New Jersey.

After assembly Molly and Tsippi went back to Miss Tuck for history, and when class was over Molly ran to the wardrobe and stood beside Tsippi, to keep Big Naomi from joining them. She thought of telling Tsippi about the chemise episode but changed her mind.

As they reached the school-yard gate, Molly covered her mouth with her hand. "You coming over to do homework?" she asked.

Tsippi shook her head. "I can't," she said.

Molly wondered why Tsippi had stopped there. Usually Tsippi said why, and supplied details. Molly waved a hand. Hunching her shoulders against the cold, she started for home. She had taken a new book out of the library and looked forward to starting it.

"Don't take off the coat," Mama said as Molly opened the door. "I want you to go to Thirteenth Avenue, to the bakery. I need a rye bread."

Molly wanted to read. She did not want to go back out again. "It's cold out, Ma," she said, hoping to get out of it.

"Then put on long stockings and a hat, like a normal person, and go," Mama said. She looked at Molly. "You see I'm busy, making supper. Why do you have to act that way? Who should I send? Rebecca? Yaaki?"

"I'll go," Rebecca said.

"Me, too," Yaaki called from the basin.

Molly felt guilty. "Oh, never mind," she said, "I'll go." She put away her schoolbag and held out her hand.

"Sliced or unsliced?" she asked.

Mama gave her ten cents. "Unsliced," she said. "It stays fresher. I can slice it myself."

Molly opened the door and went out. As she walked

down to Thirteenth Avenue, she wondered if she should stop and see Julie. Julie lived near the bakery. Molly thought better of it. She liked Julie a lot, but Mrs. Roth, her mother, was a real *kvetch*, always complaining and always pretending to be sick and wearing cold compresses on her head, so Julie would have to do all the work around the house.

Molly was surprised when she got to Thirteenth Avenue. It was as full of shoppers as if it were a warm spring evening, and people crowded around pushcarts and filled the stores. She glanced at the cakes and breads in the bakery window and went inside.

As she stood waiting for her turn, she turned to the window. On the other side of it, Tsippi and Big Naomi had suddenly appeared. Shocked, Molly watched them stop to speak with the pushcart man, just opposite the bakery. It was Big Naomi's father. Molly knew he had a pushcart on Thirteenth Avenue. She could feel her heart beating against her chest.

"Come on, girlie, people are waiting," the man behind the counter said gruffly.

Molly looked at him.

"What do you want?" he asked.

"Rye bread, unsliced," she said dully.

She took the bag he handed her, and her change as well, and moved toward the door. Standing to the side, she watched Tsippi and Naomi through the glass. When their backs were turned, she opened the door and hurried out into the crowd.

Numb with hurt, Molly headed for home.

CHAPTER SEVEN

Purim

Over the evening Molly's deep hurt turned gradually to anger. In the morning she sat at the breakfast table fuming and hoping that Tsippi would not show up. Molly couldn't stand the thought of looking at her face. Tsippi had mentioned cramps, and Molly hoped she had them and that they would keep her away.

As it happened, Molly got her wish. Tsippi did not appear. When it came time to leave for school, for the first time in a long time Molly and Rebecca walked to school alone, without her.

When Molly arrived in class, she looked straight ahead, to avoid meeting Tsippi's glance, and went directly to her seat. A moment later, Tsippi was standing beside her.

"I couldn't get up this morning," Tsippi said. "My parents had a meeting in the house last night and they were talking so loud, I couldn't fall asleep."

Molly stared at Tsippi in disbelief. Who cared about this morning? It was probably a lie, anyhow. What about yesterday afternoon? Why hadn't Tsippi said what she was doing with Big Naomi on Thirteenth Avenue, after telling Molly, her best friend, she couldn't do homework with her? Molly knew Tsippi had no way of knowing that she had been seen. But she was outraged and wanted an explanation anyhow. She couldn't say a word. She didn't have to. The starting bell rang and Tsippi hurried back to her seat.

All that day Molly successfully avoided Tsippi. If she saw her coming, she hurried away. If she caught her glance, she turned her head. In the afternoon, Tsippi left school early. Tsippi was not at school the following morning either, but she did come for the afternoon session. Once Molly failed to look away in time, and Tsippi waved from across the room.

When the bell rang at three on Friday, Molly's feelings were ajumble. Whenever Tsippi wasn't doing something with her parents on Friday nights, she came to Molly's house after supper, to hear Molly and her family sing Sabbath table songs. Molly didn't want Tsippi coming over tonight. She didn't give Tsippi a chance to say anything. Instead, Molly grabbed her coat from the wardrobe and ran home.

Molly was sure, when Tsippi did not appear on Friday night, or on Saturday afternoon, that Tsippi had finally gotten the message and would not be coming around anymore. On Sunday Molly was convinced of it. Even if Mama had invited Tsippi for *hamantaschen*, Molly didn't see how Tsippi could dare appear.

In a bad mood, Molly moped around the house all morning, going in and out of the kitchen, where Mama and Bessie had baked *hamantaschen*, the little three-cornered cakes that are eaten on Purim. In spite of herself, Molly stopped to breathe in the wonderful aroma of baking that filled the house.

Mama went up to the windowsill, where the *hamantaschen* were cooling in a pan, and felt them. "They're ready," she said, lifting them out and stacking them up on a plate.

"Here they are, the little beauties," she added, setting the plate on the table.

Molly had no appetite, but the cakes looked and smelled so good she couldn't help wanting one.

"Which are poppy seeds?" she asked, looking them over.

"On the right," Mama said. "On the left is prunes."

Yaaki and Joey came rushing out of Joey's room, where they had been reading the Sunday comics. "Did I hear someone say *hamantaschen*?" Joey asked, sniffing the air.

"Help yourself," Bessie said, smiling and showing her gold tooth and pointing to the plate.

"I can't reach it," Yaaki said.

Bessie handed him a cake.

"Leave some for the company," Mama said, watching Joey reach for a second one.

"What company?" Joey asked.

"Tsippi," Mama said.

Molly winced. "She may not come," she said, preparing the ground.

"She's not company—she's here all the time," Joey said.

Rebecca came in from the outside. She had been visiting Mrs. Chiodo, the next-door neighbor and her best friend. She waited as Mama undressed her, then rushed to the table for a *hamantasch*.

A moment later the front door opened and Papa came in.

"Look who I found in the street," he said, taking off his coat and moving aside to show Tsippi.

Tsippi stood there grinning.

Molly was dumbfounded. How dare she!

Tsippi breathed in the good smells and smiled at Molly's mother. "You invited me," she said happily, as if nothing had happened.

"Of course," Mama said. "Take off your coat."

Tsippi's glasses flew off as she removed her hat, and everyone laughed as she stood staring hungrily at the *hamantaschen*, letting Bessie pick up her glasses and take off her coat.

"Here," Joey said, giving Tsippi a *hamantasch*.

She bit into it and rolled her eyes, and everyone laughed again.

Molly stood like a statue, wondering how Tsippi could act so natural.

"Come on, people," Mama said, shepherding everyone to the table. "Let's sit down like human beings, then we'll go to the synagogue."

She poured tea for the grown-ups and milk for the children.

Molly felt like someone in a dream. She seated herself so she wouldn't have to look at Tsippi.

"Tsippi," Yaaki said, "did you bring me the present?"

Tsippi turned red. Molly realized that Tsippi had forgotten. She had forgotten too. She resented having to help Tsippi out of a pickle. But she did not want her little brother to be disappointed.

"I have it," she said, getting up. "I forgot to give it to you. Close your eyes—I'll get it."

Molly hurried to her notebook and tore out a crisp, new sheet. She rolled it up into a ball and returned to the kitchen.

"You can look now," she said, standing before Yaaki and opening her fist.

Yaaki watched the paper unroll, listening with fascination to the sound it made. Molly gave it to him and sat down.

"Ma, he didn't say thanks," Rebecca said.

"Thank you," Yaaki said to Tsippi.

Molly would have liked to spit, but she couldn't—the whole family was watching—so she answered Tsippi's grateful look with a forced smile.

Papa took a *hamantasch* from the plate. "Does everyone know what this stands for?" he asked.

"Tell us," Tsippi said, chewing away.

Molly sat like a statue.

"More than two thousand years ago, Queen Esther was married to Ahasuerus, the king of Persia," Papa began. "Her cousin, Mordekai, had once saved the king's life."

Papa paused and looked at Mama.

"Is it all right for the head of the family to take a second *hamantasch*?" he asked.

"I thought I was the head of the family," Mama said with a smile.

Molly could feel Tsippi trying to catch her eye, but she wouldn't let it happen.

"Here, Papa," Rebecca said, handing Papa a cake. "Finish the story."

"The king's minister was a cruel and hateful man," Papa said, taking a bite. "Haman was his name. Haman hated Mordekai because Mordekai would not bow down to him. And he told the king lies about the Jews and plotted to kill them. One day, Mordekai overheard . . ."

Papa paused and looked about. "Who remembers who Mordekai was?"

"Esther's cousin," Tsippi said.

Molly recoiled at the sound of her voice.

"Was he Mama's cousin too?" Rebecca asked.

Despite herself, Molly laughed along with the others. Mama's sister was named Esther.

"No, this Esther lived a long time ago," Papa said. "So where was I?" he asked.

"Mordekai overheard . . ." Tsippi said.

Molly felt disgust.

"Oh, yes," Papa said. "Mordekai overheard Haman plotting to kill the Jews, so he told the queen and the queen begged the king to save the Jews, and he did. And he had Haman hanged from a tree."

Papa glanced around the table. "The *hamantaschen* are named after Haman," he said.

"But if he was so rotten, why did they name something so delicious after him?" Tsippi asked.

Molly looked at her former best friend. How could she act as if nothing had happened?

"That's a good question," Papa said.

There was a knock on the door and Big Naomi came in.

Molly stared in disbelief.

"Hi," Big Naomi said, looking about. Her eyes came to rest on Tsippi. "I went to your house," she said. "Your mother said you were here."

Molly saw Tsippi turn red.

"Invite your friend to sit down," Mama said.

Molly pretended not to hear. Big Naomi was not her friend. Her only wish was for Big Naomi, and Tsippi, to leave. Tsippi came to the rescue.

"She can't stay," she said, getting up. "She has to go someplace, and so do I."

Tsippi pulled Big Naomi over to the closet as she went for her coat, then started for the door.

Mama turned to Molly. "At least give her a *hamantasch* to take," she said.

Molly had no objection to that. It served her plan. She took a cake from the plate and brought it to Big Naomi. Big Naomi took it and, chewing, went out.

Tsippi looked at Molly.

"I don't want to talk to you ever again," Molly whispered, and almost pushed Tsippi out.

Molly returned to her seat.

Soon, according to plan, the whole family left for the synagogue. Outside, Rebecca paused in front of Mrs. Chiodo's house. She beckoned to Mrs. Chiodo, who appeared to be waiting in the window, and Mrs. Chiodo came out.

"Rebecca invited me for the Purim," she said.

Molly could see that Mama knew nothing of it and was surprised.

"Wonderful, wonderful," Mama said, taking Mrs. Chiodo by the arm.

Molly promised herself, as she walked along, that she would get even with Tsippi, even if she wasn't sure how.

In the lobby of the synagogue Molly saw Hannah Gittel, a girl she knew, and waved to her. A lot of Jewish kids came to the synagogue on Purim for the fun, even those whose parents weren't religious, and Molly saw some other girls she knew. She went inside with her family and they all took seats. Joey was a monitor. He and another boy went up and down the aisles giving out *graggars*, noisemakers. Molly was fuming. She sat clutching her noisemaker.

Soon Mr. Persky, the Hebrew teacher, came out on-stage. He opened a scroll, *The Story of Esther*, which was read aloud at Purim, and began to read. Each time he said, "Haman," everyone in the audience hissed and booed; they stamped their feet and twirled *graggars*. Papa had explained to Mrs. Chiodo that noise was made to drown out Haman's evil name. Molly twirled her *graggar* as much for Tsippi as for Haman.

Afterward, as Molly was leaving with her family, she caught sight of Ruthie Riness and Rotten Beverly in the lobby. *Poor Ruthie*, Molly thought. *The only friend she could find to go to the synagogue with was Rotten Beverly, who everyone hates.*

"Molly!" someone called.

Molly knew it was Ruthie Riness. "Oh, hi," she said, as if she had not already seen her.

"Where's your shadow?" Beverly asked.

Molly knew she meant Tsippi. Molly never spoke to Beverly if she could help it. But suddenly she knew how to get even. Beverly was the biggest tattletale in school. Tsippi didn't want anyone to know that her parents were Communists. She was ashamed of it. Only Molly and her family knew. Communists believed in Russia. Now Russia was on America's side. But before, Russia was on Hitler's side.

"If you mean Tsippi," Molly said, "she's not my shadow. Besides, she doesn't go to the synagogue. Her parents are Communists. They don't believe in Purim, or God, or anything."

"Communists!" Beverly said. "Stinko-pinko!" she added, making a face.

Molly felt suddenly uneasy. Beverly was crazy. There was no telling what she might do.

"Molly, where are you?" Mama called in the crowd.

"Here," Molly yelled, answering into the crowd. She turned back to Ruthie.

"Is she your friend?" Molly whispered as Beverly turned to greet someone.

Ruthie shook her head. "I came with my mother and father," she said, nodding into the crowd. "I only met her here."

"If you don't ask her to go, or anybody else, I'll go with you to the restaurant," Molly said.

Ruthie looked at her. "It's a Chinese restaurant. You said your family was kosher."

"They are," Molly said. "Don't say anything."

Ruthie put a finger to her lips. "I won't."

"Molly! We're going," Mama called.

"Coming," Molly said, and went to join her family.

On the way home, Molly wondered at what she had done. She had been brought up by orthodox Jewish parents and taught to obey Jewish law and to eat only kosher food, and here she had agreed to go to a Chinese restaurant. She had heard Joey say once that they served fried cockroaches in Chinese restaurants. She shuddered. That wasn't the point. The point was her family was kosher.

She was not even allowed to eat in the house of a friend whose family was not kosher.

That night, in bed, long after Rebecca and Bessie had fallen asleep, Molly wondered about the things she had done.

CHAPTER EIGHT

Molly's Sorrow

Monday morning Molly marched into class and went right to her seat without looking around. She became aware of a buzzing as she sat down. Beverly, beside her, kept turning in her seat and whispering to the kids nearby. Molly had a sinking feeling.

"What happened?" she asked, hating to give Beverly the satisfaction of speaking to her.

Beverly turned to face her. "They're all saying Tsippi's parents are spies for Hitler," Beverly said.

Molly's heart went out of her. What had she done? Beverly was crazy. Molly should have known better. She began trembling.

Miss Tuck came away from the door as the starting bell rang and took her seat.

"It sounds like an invasion of bees in here, with all the buzzing," she said. "What is the whispering about?"

No one answered. Beverly looked up at the ceiling. Molly felt numb. She glanced over her shoulder and saw Tsippi's face, red and teary.

Miss Tuck rose and leaned over the desk, the way she did when she wanted to make a point. "Who will tell me what it is?" she said.

Molly was on the point of tears. She had to admit it. That was the least she could do. She rose at the side of her desk, trembling.

"It's my fault, Miss Tuck," she said. "I got mad at Tsippi for something and I wanted to get even. I told Beverly that Tsippi's parents were Communists. I shouldn't have, I know that, I'm sorry. But Beverly is telling everyone something different. She's saying Tsippi's parents were spies for Hitler. That's a lie, Miss Tuck. They're Jews. Hitler is killing Jews. How could they be spies for Hitler?"

Molly's knees buckled as she sat down.

"Thank you, Molly," Miss Tuck said. "We pay a big price for getting even. But I admire you for admitting your part."

Molly bit her lip to keep from crying.

Miss Tuck glanced around the room. "In this country everyone has the right to believe whatever they want," she said. "If Tsippi's parents want to be Communists, they have that right, just as other parents have the right to be Democrats, Socialists, Republicans, whatever."

She paused. "Tsippi's parents are as good patriots as the parents of anyone in this room," she said.

Molly was aware of a hush in the room. She heard a loud sniffle and saw Tsippi get her coat and run from class. Molly got up to go after her but Miss Tuck stopped her.

"Let her go," the teacher said.

She went to the wall and rolled down the wall map. "Open your geographies," she said.

All that morning, Molly heard nothing of what the teacher said. She couldn't get Tsippi's face out of her mind. Nor could she believe what she had done. Tsippi's only crime had been to befriend Big Naomi. But what she herself had done was far worse. How could she ever have been so stupid?

When the lunch bell rang, Molly got her coat and hurried out. Big Naomi caught up with her in the hall.

"Boy, that was a rotten thing to do," Big Naomi said and walked on.

Molly had no answer. Big Naomi was right. As Molly headed for the stairs, she heard Ruthie call her name. She pretended not to hear and kept going. She didn't feel like talking to anyone. Ruthie caught up with her on the stairs.

"I agree with Miss Tuck," Ruthie said. "I admire you, too."

Molly looked at her.

"For admitting your part," Ruthie said.

Molly could have cried. "It's nothing to admire," she said, and continued on down.

"I bet there's one thing that would help Tsippi feel better," Ruthie said.

Molly waited to hear what she had to say.

"You told Miss Tuck and the class, but you didn't tell Tsippi you were sorry," Ruthie said.

The picture of Tsippi's red face flashed before Molly's eyes and made her want to cry.

"Would you do me a favor?" she said with a sniffle.

"Sure," Ruthie said.

"You know my little sister, Rebecca?"

Ruthie nodded.

"She's in kindergarten," Molly said. "Could you get her and cross her at the corner?"

"Sure," Ruthie said.

"Tell her to tell my mother I'll be right home—I had to go to Tsippi's house for a minute."

"Okay," Ruthie said, and went around the stairs to the kindergarten.

Molly left the school yard and went across the street, to the apartment building where Tsippi lived. She hurried up the stairs to Tsippi's floor and rang Tsippi's bell.

Tsippi came to the door. "What do you want?" she asked, red eyed.

"I want to say I'm sorry," Molly said.

"Did Miss Tuck send you?" Tsippi asked.

"Nobody sent me. I came myself," Molly said.

Tsippi looked at her, then closed the door. Molly could hear crying.

Brokenhearted, Molly went down the stairs.

Molly could not get Tsippi's face out of her mind all day. That night, in bed, she waited for Rebecca and Bessie to fall asleep, then cried and cried into her pillow.

CHAPTER NINE

Shabbos

Molly tried several times during the week to apologize again to Tsippi, but without success. The tables had turned. Now it was Tsippi walking away whenever Molly came near.

At home Molly sensed that Mama and Bessie wondered why they didn't see Tsippi anymore. Rebecca never brought it up, but Molly knew she was curious too. Finally, Friday night after supper, when for the second time Tsippi didn't show up to hear the *Shabbos* songs, Mama brought the subject up.

"Why don't we see Tsippi anymore?" she asked as she removed the dishes from the table. Bessie, Rebecca, and Yaaki were still seated there. Papa was in the living room, reading, and Joey had gone out with his friends.

Molly had grown accustomed to the silence surrounding Tsippi and was taken by surprise.

"She—she's busy," she said.

She saw Mama and Bessie exchange glances.

"I think they had a fight," Rebecca said.

Molly shot her sister a look.

"Did you?" Mama asked.

"No," Molly said. "It's just that she lives right across from the school. Why should she walk all the way over here every day?"

Mama looked at her. "She always lived there, and you

always lived here, but she came every day anyhow," she said.

Molly didn't know what to say.

"She used to come Friday all the time," Bessie said.

"I told you," Rebecca said. "I think they had a fight."

Molly was grateful that Yaaki, at least, said nothing. He just sat there and listened.

"Wrong," she said, getting up. "We see each other in school all the time. Look," she added, glancing from one to the other, "I'm not the only person in the world, and neither is she. She has other friends, and so do I."

As she spoke, she was aware that her family had not met any new friends.

"As a matter of fact," she added, "one is coming over tomorrow. Ruthie is her name."

"I know her—she came to get me," Rebecca said.

"Right," Molly said, glad to have proof of Ruthie's existence.

"It's the same name as my doll," Rebecca said.

"I know," Molly said, and looked away. She felt terrible. All her thoughts were distressful. Tsippi; telling Ruthie she would go to the Chinese restaurant; making up lies . . .

On Saturday, when her father came home from the synagogue, Molly began to feel a little better. The big *Shabbos* meal, and the songs of praise and thanksgiving, lifted her spirits. Afterward, she went to Ruthie's house, brought her back home, and introduced her to everyone in the family.

Rebecca was at the door, on the way out. "I'm going to see Mrs. Chiodo," she said.

"Who's Mrs. Chiodo?" Ruthie asked as Rebecca left.

"Her best friend, an Italian lady who lives next door," Molly said.

"She's cute," Ruthie said. Her eyes went to Yaaki. "But he's beautiful," she added, full of admiration.

Molly felt uncomfortable, alone with Ruthie. "Let's go see Julie," she said.

"Okay," Ruthie said with her usual readiness to go along. "What happened with Tsippi?" she asked as they went out onto the stoop.

Molly wondered why Ruthie hadn't asked earlier. She guessed she was being polite. "She wouldn't talk to me," Molly said. "She closed the door."

Ruthie looked up at the sky. "It's getting nice out," she said.

Molly agreed. The day was quite mild and the girls strolled down to Thirteenth Avenue. Standing on the sidewalk in front of Julie's house, Molly called up to her.

Julie came to the window. "I'll be right down," she said.

Julie came out wearing a winter coat that was way too big for her.

"My mother doesn't feel well," she said, blowing her frizzy red hair out of her eyes. "I can't stay long."

Molly introduced the girls; then they all sat down on some boxes that had been put out in front of a store.

"It's her birthday tomorrow," Molly said, nodding at Ruthie.

"Oh, happy birthday," Julie said. "How old are you?"

"Eleven," Ruthie said.

"I'll be eleven in November," Molly said. "I skipped the third grade."

"I'm eleven too," Julie said. "You know what else it says on my birth certificate?" she asked.

"What?" Molly asked.

Julie giggled. "I never told anyone before," she said. "Julie is not my real name."

"What is?" Molly asked, surprised.

Julie made a face. "Julius," she answered with an embarrassed smile, and blew the hair out of her eyes.

"But that's a boy's name," Molly said.

"I know. My mother named me after her father. The kids in school used to make fun of me and make me cry. Mrs. Wissoff took pity on me and started calling me Julie. And that's how I got the name," she said with a smile.

"It's a nice name," Ruthie said.

"Even my mother calls me that now," Julie said.

Some mother, Molly thought.

In the same moment Mrs. Roth came to the window.

"Julie," she called. "Get a quarter pound sliced salami and four slices bread. Here's money," she added, and threw a handkerchief with some coins out the window.

Julie ran to pick it up. "I better go," she said. "She's not feeling well," she repeated.

Molly watched Julie walk away. She felt sorry for Julie. On *Shabbos*, when everyone was supposed to eat a delicious Sabbath meal, Julie's mother fed her a salami sandwich.

The sun was beginning to go down, and Molly and Ruthie headed back. They discussed Sunday as they walked up Forty-third Street.

"I'll tell my mother I'm going to your house to do

homework," she said. "What time am I supposed to come to the restaurant?"

"My father said three o'clock," Ruthie said. She looked at Molly. "Are you sure it's all right for you to go?"

Molly did not answer. It wasn't all right. In fact it was all wrong. It was a sin. But she had promised to go, and she would go.

"I told my parents about it," Ruthie said. "Not about you," she added quickly. "I said it was another girl. They said if the girl ate chicken, it wouldn't be so bad. Chicken is kosher."

Molly knew about kosher. She had watched her mother kosher a chicken every Friday. "It's only kosher if a Jewish butcher kills it," she said, "and if you put salt on it to let the blood drain out."

"Well," Ruthie said, "so long as you don't eat pork. That's really not kosher."

"Pork!" Molly repeated. "I wouldn't eat pork in a million years."

They arrived at Molly's stoop.

"See you tomorrow," Molly said, going sadly up the steps.

CHAPTER TEN

The Chinese Restaurant

Sunday morning Papa went out for papers, *The Daily News* for the children, so they could read the jokes, and the Jewish paper for the grown-ups. He sat at the kitchen table reading. Bessie, next to him, sat sewing a hem, and Mama was washing clothes on the washboard in the kitchen sink. Joey had gone into his room with the jokes, and Rebecca and Yaaki were in there with him.

Everyone but Molly was occupied. She was too restless to sit still. Her thoughts churned. She walked back and forth, from Joey's room to the kitchen to the living room to her bedroom back to Joey's room. She couldn't get the picture of Tsippi crying out of her mind. If she managed to wipe it away for an instant, she was disturbed by the thought of the Chinese restaurant, the lies, the sin.

Trying once more, she took her library book out and sat down with it again. Suddenly, out of the blue, she had an idea: If she wrote Tsippi a letter, Tsippi would have to read it. She couldn't walk away from a letter. She couldn't slam the door on it. On Sundays Tsippi often went for a ride in the car with her parents, to visit relatives. Molly could slip the letter under her door.

Molly jumped at the idea. She took out her notebook and began to write. She copied the letter again and again until she had it right. Then she copied it for a last time onto a clean page.

Dear Tsippi, she wrote. *I didn't think that Beverly would do that. She is even worse than I thought. I didn't mean to hurt you. I just wanted to get even. Getting even doesn't pay, I know that now. But when I saw you on Thirteenth Avenue with Big Naomi, it hurt me. And when you had her meet you at my house, that was too much.*

As Miss Tuck said, "We pay a big price for getting even." I am paying a big price. I AM MISERABLE. I hope you will forgive me because I am very sorry. I hope we can be friends again.

Molly didn't know how to end the letter. She couldn't say, *Your best friend*. And she didn't feel right saying, *Yours truly*, the ending she had learned in school. Finally she just signed her name, and added, *P.S. I'm really, really sorry. PLEASE FORGIVE ME.*

Feeling better, Molly folded the letter and put on her coat.

"Ma, I'm going to Tsippi's house," she said, glad to be speaking the truth, even if it didn't mean what it sounded like.

Mama looked up from the sink. "Be on time for lunch," she said.

Molly went up the street, to Tsippi's house. She looked up and down the block where Tsippi lived but saw no sign of her father's car. The coast was clear. She hurried up the stairs and slipped the letter under Tsippi's door.

When she came down, she was too excited to go home. She went to Thirteenth Avenue to see Julie again and called to her from the sidewalk. Julie came to the window.

"I can't come down. Come up," she said, motioning.

Molly didn't want to go up. But she wasn't ready yet to go home either. Grudgingly, she climbed the stairs. To her surprise, she found Nice Beverly in Julie's house.

The two girls were sitting in the kitchen. Mrs. Roth was in her usual position, lying on the couch in the living room with a cold compress on her head and listening to the radio. Molly did not mean to stay long and so did not take off her coat. She sat in the kitchen with Julie and Beverly for a while talking about P.S. 164, then said she had to go.

"See you tomorrow," Julie and Beverly called after her.

Molly imagined, as she walked home, that a letter from Tsippi was waiting for her. She knew it was impossible—she had dropped off her own letter only a short while ago—but she liked the thought.

When she got home, she found everyone seated around the kitchen table eating lunch and listening to the president on the radio. Mama's friend Goldie was there too. Molly took off her coat and sat with them. Sandwich food was out on the table: cold cuts, bread, pickles, olives, and mustard. Sunday was delicatessen day. Mothers didn't cook then. Molly thought sadly about Julie's meal yesterday. Mrs. Roth, Julie's mother, gave Julie delicatessen food on *Shabbos*.

Molly looked at the clock. She was in a quandary. She would soon be going out to eat. How could she eat now? Yet if she didn't eat, it would look suspicious. She took a green olive, ate it, and put the pit on her plate.

"My fellow Americans," the president said. "As I told Congress yesterday, *sacrifice* is not the proper word with which to describe this program of self-denial. When, at the end of this great struggle, we shall have saved our way of life, we shall have made no 'sacrifice.' The price for civilization must be paid in hard work and sorrow and blood. The price is not too high. If you doubt it, ask those millions who live today under the tyranny of Hitlerism. Ask the women and children whom Hitler is starving whether the rationing of tires and gasoline and sugar is too great a sacrifice."

Molly was on the point of tears. For a long time, only the Jews were against Hitler. Now even the president was speaking against him.

Papa turned off the radio and Mama got up and brought the teapot and glasses to the table.

"He's a great man, that Franklin Delanor Roosevelt," she said, pouring tea.

"Not Delanor, Ma," Joey said. "Dela*no*."

"I hear everyone say Delanor," Mama said.

"The wife, Mrs. Roosevelt, her name is Eleanor," Papa said.

"It sounds the same to me," Mama said, leaning over the table to fill Bessie's glass.

"No, Ma, listen," Joey said. "One is del-a-NO. The other is el-a-NOR."

"Where's the difference?" Mama said. "Franklin Delanor Roosevelt. That's what I said."

"Leave her alone," Goldie said, sipping from her glass. "Her English is good enough, better than Goldie's."

Molly glanced at the clock on the shelf. It was time for her to leave. She swallowed hard, hoping there would be no questions.

"Ma, I'm going to Ruthie's house. We have to memorize something for school," she said.

"You didn't eat anything," Mama said.

Molly pointed to the pit on her plate. "I did," she said.

"She seems like a nice girl, this Ruthie," Mama said.

"Very nice," Bessie added.

It made Molly feel good to hear them approve of Ruthie. She wondered. She did not consider her a friend, not really. But then who was? Julie was stuck at home, with her mother. Big Naomi was no longer her friend. Little Naomi lived too far. Nice Beverly seemed to keep to herself. Now that she thought of it, right now Ruthie was her only friend.

"She has a straight part in her hair," Rebecca said.

Molly looked at her sister, surprised. Rebecca noticed everything.

"Don't come back late," Mama said.

"I'll be home before Eddie Cantor," Molly said, getting into her coat, relieved that it had gone so easily.

Once she got outside, she felt uneasy again. What if she were caught? What if someone saw her? She was frightened as she walked to Thirteenth Avenue. When she arrived at the restaurant, she couldn't bring herself to go in for a while. She stood looking in the window of the dress store next door, watching the street. When she saw no one she knew and felt she had not been seen, she opened the door and hurried into the restaurant.

"Molly!" Ruthie called from a table in back.

Molly's hands were sweaty as she walked to the rear. She stood stiffly at the edge of the table where Ruthie was sitting with her parents. Yesterday, at Ruthie's house, she had barely spoken to Mr. Riness. Mrs. Riness had not been at home. Now Ruthie introduced them.

"Sit down," Mr. Riness said, indicating the chair next to Ruthie.

Molly had almost forgotten to say it. "Happy birthday," she said.

"Thanks," Ruthie said, beaming.

Molly was surprised to learn, when she heard Mr. and Mrs. Riness speak, that they were immigrants and had heavy Jewish accents, like her own mother and father. She had imagined, since they ate in restaurants, that they were Americans.

Molly glanced around to see what a restaurant was like. Chinese waiters in red jackets moved between the tables, bringing food. Behind Mrs. Riness, on the door, the word *Ladies* was written. Molly supposed it was a girls' bathroom, like the ones in school.

A waiter came to the table with a pad and pencil.

"My daughter will have the combination plate," Mr. Riness said. He leaned toward Molly. "Ruthie said you like chicken."

Molly glanced at Ruthie and nodded.

"Chicken chow mein for this young lady," Mr. Riness said.

Molly felt guilty. It made no difference what she ate. The restaurant wasn't kosher.

Mrs. Riness put down the menu she had been studying. "I'll have sweet and sour pork," she said to the waiter.

Molly was flabbergasted. Pork? Mrs. Riness was an immigrant, like Mama. Her Jewish accent was even worse than Mama's. How could she sit there and order pork, like the *goyim*?

The waiter returned with plates of food. Molly recoiled at the sight of the dish that had been placed before her.

It looked like a hill of worms. She even thought she saw one move.

"What did you get?" she asked Ruthie, turning away from the sight.

Ruthie touched each thing on her plate with her fork. "This is egg roll, this is chow mein, same as yours, and this is fried rice," she said.

Molly noticed that everyone was eating and took up her fork. She didn't know if her hand shook or the food was slippery, but it slid off the fork before she could get it to her mouth. She tried again. This time she made it. She tried to keep a normal expression on her face to hide her disgust. It not only looked like worms, it tasted that way.

"Do you like it?" Ruthie asked.

Molly managed a smile as she fought back nausea.

"Is everything all right?" Mr. Riness asked Molly.

She managed another smile.

"Don't you like it?" Ruthie asked.

Molly swallowed. "Oh, yeah," she said, trying to put some enthusiasm into her voice. She thought she had spotted pieces of chicken in the plate. With her fork, she turned the food over until she found some chicken bits and brought another forkful to her mouth. The chicken tasted exactly like the other stuff. Another wave of nausea.

Molly was glad Mr. Riness was talking about his laundry business. She wondered, since she had had two bites, if she could say she was full. She decided she couldn't, not yet. Food was expensive. Mr. Riness was paying out good money.

Ruthie started speaking about Miss Tuck, and glad

for the opportunity to put her fork down and listen, Molly gave Ruthie all her attention. Soon everyone was busy chewing again, and Molly found herself the only one not eating. Molly saw Mrs. Riness look at her and quickly put another bit of food in her mouth.

She shouldn't have done it. Nausea swelled up, filling her throat. She was going to be sick. With no thought to what Mrs. Riness might say or how much the meal cost, she ran to the ladies' room and hung her head over a bowl.

Ruthie came running in. "Are you all right, Molly?"

Molly could not speak. Her insides were tossing like the waves of the ocean.

"Is it on account of the food?" Ruthie said.

Molly shook her head as best she could. She heaved, but nothing came up. Some woman came in from the restaurant, bringing a rush of fresh air with her. The air relieved Molly. She stood up to test herself. The nausea was there but she did not think anymore that she would throw up.

"Are you okay?" Ruthie asked.

Molly swallowed to see. She gave a small nod and went to the sink. She turned on the tap and took a mouthful of water. As she swirled the water from cheek to cheek, she studied the details of the ladies' room, sure she would never see it again. When she spat out, she felt better. Still queasy, but better.

"Okay?" Ruthie said.

Molly nodded.

Ruthie opened the door and Molly followed her out, looking neither right nor left, trying to avoid the sight of food. Mr. and Mrs. Riness were near the door, holding the coats.

"Is she all right?" Mrs. Riness asked Ruthie, as if Molly weren't there.

"Uh-huh," Ruthie said.

"Come," Mr. Riness said, handing the girls their coats. "We'll walk Molly home."

On the way out, Molly squeezed herself between Ruthie's parents so as not to be seen. Holding her stomach, suspicious of the feeling in her throat, she walked home in silence.

She was afraid to speak but didn't want to be impolite. "Thank you, Mr. and Mrs. Riness," she said in a small voice when she got to her house. Slowly, she turned to Ruthie. "I hope I didn't spoil your birthday," she added.

"You didn't," Ruthie said. "I was glad I had a friend with me."

"We hope you feel better," Mr. Riness said.

Molly nodded. "I do," she said weakly.

"Let's go," Mrs. Riness said. "Her mother will take care of her."

"Good-bye," Ruthie called over her shoulder, following her parents home.

Molly watched Ruthie go. She wondered, as she went up the stoop, if Tsippi had delivered a letter. She was about to go in and find out, but a new wave of nausea flared up, and she opened her mouth and stuck out her tongue, to let the cold air rush in and stop it.

She felt wretched. She had never known what it meant to be nauseous before. But she did not feel sorry for herself. She deserved it. She had plotted against Tsippi, she had lied, she had broken the commandment that said, *Honor thy father and thy mother*, and she had further sinned by eating nonkosher food. She deserved to be punished. And she was willing to accept it. But if the punishment was mostly for eating nonkosher food, she hoped that God knew she did it for poor Ruthie's sake and hoped also that God had noticed how much she had eaten: hardly anything, two bites, not even, that was all.

Holding her stomach, with a quick smile at heaven to show God she wasn't angry about the punishment, she went in.

CHAPTER ELEVEN

Yaaki Has a Tantrum

As she hung up her coat, she saw with relief that only Papa and Yaaki were at home. They didn't notice things the way Mama did. She ducked into the bathroom and rinsed her mouth, swirling, swirling, washing away the nausea. She swallowed, feeling better, and went into the living room, hoping against hope that the nausea would be completely gone by the time Mama came home.

Yaaki was sitting on the floor in his basin, puffing out his cheeks and making airplane noises, and Papa was in the easy chair, struggling to put just the right amount of tobacco on a tiny piece of paper. Since the war had started, he couldn't buy regular cigarettes; they were for the soldiers.

Molly looked around in all the logical places but saw no letter from Tsippi.

"Did anyone come to call for me?" she asked.

"No one," Papa said, carefully rolling the cigarette.

"Where's Mama?"

"She went with Bessie to visit Tillie," Yaaki answered.

"Rebecca too?" Molly asked.

Papa nodded and lit the crooked cigarette.

Molly swallowed, testing herself again. So far so good. The idea of a dry piece of bread felt right to her, and she went to the bread box in the kitchen and snipped off a piece. At first she thought she had made a mistake and that something was going to happen. But the bread went down and stayed down and seemed even to act as a lid on the nausea. She took another piece and ate it. She was hungry.

Molly took out her library book and sat with it on the couch as if she were reading. She swallowed and breathed, swallowed and breathed. The nausea seemed to be going, but she had the feeling that she was being watched. When she looked up she saw that it was only Jabotinsky, looking down at her from his picture on the wall.

The door opened and Mama came in with Bessie and Rebecca.

"Hi," Yaaki called from the basin.

"Hi," they all answered, gathering at the closet to put away their coats.

Molly had a pang of guilt seeing Mama, but she brushed it away, reminding herself that she had suffered and been punished. To distract herself, she looked at her aunt. Bessie was wearing her new disguise, a pair of eyeglasses from the five-and-ten and a hat with a large brim, which she pulled down over her eyes. Bessie had started wearing the disguise ever since Heshy had surprised her in the street a few days ago. He had followed her, trying to talk to her, but she didn't want to have anything to do with him. Molly did not understand why he was following Bessie if he had a new girl friend. She also didn't understand how Bessie could see where she was going, with the brim pulled down.

She decided to tease her aunt. "Who are you hiding from?" she said, as if she didn't know.

"The Germans," Bessie answered as she reached into the closet to hang up her coat.

Everyone looked up. Molly knew her aunt had meant to be funny, but what she said hadn't been taken that way.

"Bessie," Mama said, "you'll scare the children."

Molly saw Rebecca move away from the door.

Bessie looked ashamed. "The Germans can't come to Borough Park," she said, glancing from Yaaki to Rebecca to Molly. "The great American Army would never let them."

Molly knew Bessie was trying to make the children feel better. She *was* feeling better, back in her own home. She went to her room to put the book away. It was Sunday, when the good programs were on, and the family would soon be listening to the radio.

In her room were two windows. One was reserved for her conversations with God. She went up to the other. Closing her eyes, concentrating hard, she sent Tsippi a mental message. "Dear friend. I miss you. Please come to my house," she said.

When she went back out to the living room, she found Bessie and Rebecca seated on the couch, playing cat's cradle. Rebecca stopped playing and sat staring at Molly, trying to figure out what Molly had been doing in the room. Molly decided to give Rebecca something to think about. As if she were chewing on a huge wad of gum, Molly moved her jaw up and down. Rebecca would never ask. She would try to figure out what Molly could be chewing. Moving her jaw in an exaggerated way, Molly stood over Rebecca and Bessie, watching.

"Coming!" Molly heard Mama call in the kitchen.

Molly knew what it meant. Mrs. Baumfeld, the lady upstairs, had called Mama to the phone.

"Come on, Rebecca," Bessie said, waiting for Rebecca to take the string.

Papa's voice came from behind his newspaper. "France, Czechoslovakia, Poland, Russia, the Germans are everywhere! Hitler. A killer, a madman. Who could believe that such a maniac could conquer Europe?"

"God will help," Bessie said.

"Amen," Molly said, chewing hard.

Rebecca stared at Molly's mouth.

Bessie dropped the string. "If you don't want to play, I have other things to do," she said, getting up.

Molly slid into her vacated seat. "I'll play," she said, chewing and taking up the string.

"Bessie," Yaaki said, "if they won't let you play, I'll play with you."

"Thanks," Bessie said, "but I'll go straighten up Joey's room. . . ."

"You go," Molly said to Rebecca, holding up the string. Her heart stood still as she heard the front door open, but when she looked she saw only Goldie, Mama's friend.

"Hello, hello," Goldie said, marching into the living room. "Who's home?"

Papa looked up from his paper. "Laya will be down soon," he said, and went back to reading.

Chewing wildly, Molly leaned over to speak to Rebecca. "Keep playing, or she'll start talking to us," she whispered.

Rebecca looked at Molly's fingers, considering her move.

Bessie came running in. "Goldie," she said, "I thought I heard your voice. Laya went upstairs, to the phone."

As Molly, never forgetting to chew, waited for Rebecca

to make her move, she watched Goldie put a hand on her hip and twirl herself about. "*Nu*, how does Goldie look?" Goldie said.

Molly could see that Bessie was at a loss. "Did you lose weight?" Bessie asked, not understanding what Goldie meant.

"What weight?" Goldie said. "I'm talking about the haircut. Goldie has a new haircut."

Bessie glanced at Molly. "Oh yeah, I see now," she said. "You look like Mary Astor."

Goldie smiled, showing a gold tooth on either side of her mouth.

Molly leaned over to Rebecca. "Watch," she said, chewing, "she's going to ask if we have cake."

"Come into the kitchen," Bessie said. "I'll make tea."

"Did Laya bake cake this week?" Goldie asked.

Molly and Rebecca giggled.

Goldie turned to them. "Oh, hello children," she said. "Did Goldie say something funny?"

"Rebecca dropped the string by mistake," Molly said, making up a story. She was chewing hard and trying not to laugh.

Goldie stopped to look at Yaaki. "And this beautiful boy," she said, going toward him.

"No kisses," he said, raising his shoulder.

"Not even for Goldie?"

Yaaki shook his head. "I'm too busy," he said, and began shuffling the strips of paper in his basin.

Mama returned. "Guess what," she said, entering the living room. "Hello, Goldie," she added in the same breath.

Molly looked up.

"Esther and her new husband and Mordi will be here for the *seder* on Passover, but not Selma. Selma joined the WAACs!" she said.

"What's the WAACs?" Molly asked.

"The ladies' army," Papa answered.

"Selma?" Goldie asked. "Isn't that your sister's daughter, the Communist?"

"Communist-shmommunist, she doesn't know what she is," Mama said.

"She only wants to make the world better," Papa said.

"Come, we'll have tea," Mama said, leading the way to the kitchen.

Chewing, Molly watched them go. When she turned back, she caught her sister straining to look into her mouth. Molly made her move. "Boo!" she cried, opening her mouth to show it was empty.

Rebecca flinched. Yaaki let out a scream. Too late, Molly realized how careless she had been. What all the family feared had happened. She had frightened Yaaki. His body was rigid, his eyes shut tight, his mouth open. The house shook with his cries.

Mama and the others came running. *"Oy!"* Mama said, and got down on the floor beside Yaaki. She dared not touch him, not while his howls were so great. He would scream even more. She would have to wait until he spent himself, until the cries were more normal. "Hurry, bring paper," she whispered.

Molly's heart beat with fear. Around her everyone, Papa, Bessie, even Goldie, ran looking for paper to shred into the basin, in the hope that the sound and the movement would distract him. She remembered seeing the jokes in Joey's room and ran to get them.

"Look, Yaaki," she said, "*Dick Tracy*, *Little Orphan Annie*, and look, your favorite, *Little Lulu*. . . ."

Yaaki continued screaming.

"My God, he's getting blue," Mama said, clasping and unclasping her hands.

Shaking with fear, Molly tried again. "*Little Lulu*," she said pleadingly, weakly. Rebecca, on the floor beside her, swirled the papers in the basin, a frightened look on her face. Papa, Bessie, and Goldie stood or crouched, watching helplessly.

Molly remembered that Yaaki had liked the sheet from the notebook she had given him the other day and ran to get one. Writing paper was harder than newspaper and made more of a sound.

Her heart went out to her little brother when she returned. He was wet with perspiration, his curls were flat against his head. The shirt stuck to his chest. The sight was almost more than she could bear. He had been sick once, with asthma, and had suffered enough. Numb with fear, she crumpled the paper near his ear.

"God be praised," Mama whispered as he took a tiny breath.

The more he could be distracted, the quicker his cries would begin to slow down. Molly hurried to distract him again, crumpling and uncrumpling the paper at his ear. To God, she said, "Please make him stop crying. Don't let him die. If you make him stop crying, I promise to eat kosher food for the rest of my life." To Yaaki, she said, "It's a nice sound, what a nice sound, just listen. . . ."

Rebecca helped. "It's a nice sound, Yaaki," she said, shoving the papers in the basin around so he would hear still more sounds.

Yaaki took a second breath. Another break in the endless wail.

Mama tried. "Come to Mama, Yaaki," she said softly, holding out her arms to him.

He couldn't move yet.

"Look, Yaaki, *Little Lulu*," Molly repeated, crumpling paper with one hand and with the other holding up the comic sheet.

Sobbing, his chest heaving, he turned to look.

"Blessed is the Lord," Mama said.

Everyone drew a breath.

"Want me to read it to you?" Molly asked, desperate to hold his attention.

Sobbing, he tried to nod.

"Little Lulu is sitting in a room with her aunt . . ." Molly began.

"He's breathing," Papa said.

"The blueness is going," Bessie said.

"Poor thing," Goldie said.

"Thank God," Mama said.

She tried again. "Come to Mama, Yaaki," she said, opening her arms.

Sobbing, he fell into her arms. She helped him out of the basin and held him. Worn out with crying, his head resting on her chest, wet through and through, he lay staring up at the ceiling, trying to catch his breath.

The front door opened and Joey came in. He could see into the living room. "Oh, no," he said softly, recognizing the signs.

Yaaki turned wet blue eyes on Joey.

"Hi, Yaaki," Joey said in the fake cheerful voice everyone used when Yaaki had a tantrum.

Rocking Yaaki, swaying with him, holding him close, Mama looked up. "What scared him?" she asked softly.

"Molly," Rebecca answered.

Molly was on the point of tears. "I didn't mean it," she said, burning with shame.

"Molly, by now you should know that you have to watch your step," Papa said gently, but in a warning voice.

Molly looked at Yaaki. The tantrum was over. She went into her room and closed the door. She cared nothing for what any of them said. Tsippi didn't matter and neither did anything else. All she knew was that her baby brother was not going to die.

She opened God's window.

"Thank you, God," she said, gazing heavenward, and wept with relief.

CHAPTER TWELVE

Joey's Song

Molly sat at the breakfast table, watching Yaaki in his basin on the floor. She had given him her rubber-band ball last night, and he sat moving it around and under the piles of shredded paper in the basin, as if it were a ship. She was grateful to see him playing happily. She was also sad. Last night, when the house was quiet again, everyone sat down to listen to the radio. Eddie Cantor came and went. No Tsippi. No answering letter. Nothing.

"You look tired, Molly," Mama said. "You didn't sleep well?"

Molly found it hard to look Mama in the eye. "No, I slept fine," she said, sipping her cocoa.

Yaaki got up out of the basin. "Where is the book you gave me, Molly?" he asked, referring to the old workbook she had also given him.

She glanced around and saw it. "There, on the shelf," she said.

Yaaki took the book from the shelf, along with his broken flute and a crayon. "I'm going to read—no noise, please," he said, going into the living room.

"You can't read," Rebecca called after him.

"If you don't make noise, I can," he said, seating himself on the couch.

Molly smiled to herself, aware he was imitating her. She looked away and thought of school and wondered what the day would bring.

"I'm ready," Rebecca said, wiping her mouth and getting up. Rebecca was always ready. She had hung her snowsuit on the knob of the closet door and put her tin box and galoshes on the floor.

Molly looked at the galoshes. "What are those for?" she asked.

"It snowed," Rebecca said.

Molly couldn't believe it. The weather had been getting warmer. She ran to the window and looked out. A light snow covered the ground. "How can it snow?" she asked, offended. "It'll soon be Passover."

"Go sue City Hall," Mama said, glancing into the living room to see how Yaaki was doing.

Molly got dressed and helped Rebecca into her snowsuit.

The stoop was covered with a thin, powdery snow, and Molly took Rebecca by the hand and led her down.

"You saw Tsippi yesterday," Rebecca said. "I thought she was coming today, like before."

Molly was taken aback. She had said she was going to Tsippi's house. But she had not seen Tsippi. "No," she said. "Look," she added, eager to change the subject. "See the gold star in Mrs. Safir's window?"

Rebecca glanced up. "Is it for good behavior?" she asked.

"No," Molly said. "It's from the president of the United States. Remember Jerry Safir, a tall boy with curly brown hair?"

Rebecca nodded.

"He was killed in the war. The gold star means a boy in this family was killed in the war," Molly said.

"How come we don't have a gold star?" Rebecca asked.

Molly looked at her, surprised. "Why should we? No one in our family was killed."

"What about Mama's and Papa's relatives in Europe, that Hitler killed?" Rebecca asked.

The light at the corner had turned green and Molly hurried Rebecca across the street.

"The gold star is for an American, a soldier or sailor who was killed in the war," she said.

As she arrived at the school-yard gate, Molly glanced longingly at the door of Tsippi's house across the way, then marched Rebecca through the school yard and into the building. Rebecca went around the stairs to her room, and Molly went up to room 323. She felt nervous as she entered. Her eyes met Tsippi's briefly, then Tsippi glanced away.

Molly hoped, as she stood at the wardrobe, that Tsippi would come up to her; but instead Ruthie Riness was suddenly at her side.

"How do you feel?" Ruthie asked.

Reminded, Molly's stomach lurched. "Better," she said, swallowing.

"My parents were worried," Ruthie said.

"I'm okay," Molly said, anxious for Ruthie to go away, in case Tsippi was intending to approach. The ring of the bell ended Molly's uncertainty. She and Ruthie both went to their seats.

Tsippi's behavior was the same as before. It was as if Molly had never written to her. Molly waited all day, hoping Tsippi would say something to her, but Tsippi never did. When the bell rang at three o'clock, Molly saw Tsippi leave with Big Naomi. Sadly, Molly went out into the hall. Ruthie Riness caught up with her.

"What a shame, you and Tsippi are mad at each other," Ruthie said. "You used to be such good friends."

Molly was half annoyed with Ruthie. But she was glad to have someone to talk to. "I wrote her a letter yesterday, but she never answered. And she wouldn't look at me today," she added.

"Maybe she will tomorrow," Ruthie said.

"Maybe," Molly said, wondering, feeling a little better.

When Molly arrived home and saw a letter on the kitchen table, her heart leaped.

"Is the letter for me?" she asked.

Mama wiped her hands on her apron. "My brother in Palestine," she said. "Hanna had a new baby, a girl. You have a new cousin," she said.

Molly didn't care. It wasn't the answer she had hoped for. She took out her notebook to do her homework and sat down at the kitchen table.

Mama removed a bowl of chopped meat from the refrigerator and began slapping it into a loaf. Yaaki came in from the living room and sat down at the table, next to Molly. She leaned over and gave him a kiss.

"Don't," he said, wiping his cheek on his shoulder.

"Where's Rebecca?" Molly asked.

"Where is she ever when she's not here?" Mama said. "Next door, by Mrs. Chiodo."

A short while later, the front door opened and Rebecca came in, crying. The last time Molly had seen her sister bawl that way was when she had taken her to the movies for the first time and the roar of the MGM lion on the screen had scared her.

"What is it?" Mama asked, hurrying to Rebecca.

"That girl—I just saw her—" Rebecca said between sobs.

Molly put her arm around Yaaki, to assure him that Rebecca's tears were nothing to worry about. He didn't seem concerned; he looked on calmly.

"What happened?" Mama said, seating herself and pulling Rebecca toward her.

"When I left—Mrs. Chiodo's house—I saw her—the girl with the b-big head," Rebecca said between sobs.

Mama clapped a hand to her face. *"Oy!"* she said. *"Nebech,* poor girl."

Molly shuddered. The girl had a huge head that swung from side to side as she walked. The people in the neighborhood called it a water head.

"But why should you cry?" Mama asked. "She didn't touch you."

"I got s-scared," Rebecca said.

"But she didn't touch you," Mama repeated.

"Her brother was with her," Rebecca said, and started to cry all over again. "He called me a bottle baby," she said.

Molly wondered what Rebecca was talking about.

"Is what?" Mama said. "You're still a little girl. You're allowed to drink from a bottle."

Molly was baffled. She hadn't seen Rebecca drink from a bottle for a very long time.

"Is that true?" she asked.

Rebecca looked at her with wet eyes. "I drink it in the closet," she said. "Mama gives it to me when nobody sees."

Mama turned to Molly. "She made me promise not to tell. Nobody knows—except Joey—he saw once." A questioning look crossed her face. "Who is this boy?" she asked. "How could he know such a thing?"

Molly knew the boy. "He goes to Montauk. He's in Joey's class," she said.

Mama looked shocked. "Joey promised never to tell," she said.

"He told your secret, too," Rebecca said.

"Mine?" Mama asked, surprised.

Molly was dumbfounded. Did Mama drink from a bottle in the closet too? "What secret?" she asked, puzzled.

"She hides in the closet when it thunders," Rebecca said.

Molly knew that—everyone did. That was no secret.

Mama stood up. She was furious. "That's how he talks about his mother in school? Wait till I get my hands on that boy," she said.

"No hitting," Yaaki said, going into the living room with his broken plastic flute.

"Don't worry, I won't hit him," Mama said. She gave the meat loaf a hard slap and put it in the oven.

Molly wished, when she saw Joey open the door, that she could warn her brother.

"Hi," Joey called, taking off his coat.

Mama put her hands on her hips. "That's how you talk about your mother!" she said.

Joey looked bewildered. "What did I do?" he asked.

Molly felt sorry for her brother.

"You told someone I hide in the closet when it thunders?" Mama said.

"He called me a bottle baby, too," Rebecca said, her chin quivering.

Joey glanced from Mama to Rebecca. "What are you talking about? I never told anybody anything."

"The girl with water on her head. Molly says her brother is in your class," Mama said.

Molly did not want to be put in the middle. "Me? What have I got to do with it?" she asked.

Joey looked pale. "I never told him anything. Wait a minute," he said, and paused. "Once, in class, we were talking about secrets. I said I heard about a lady who hid in the closet when it thundered, and a schoolgirl who drank from a bottle in the closet because she didn't want her brothers and sisters to know."

He looked at Mama. "But I never said it was you," he said.

"I'm only in kindergarten," Rebecca said, and began to cry again.

Mama turned her back on Joey and marched into the living room. Rebecca went up to Joey, smacked him in the hip, and followed Mama.

"I never said it was you! I swear!" Joey hollered after them. He went to his room and slammed the door.

Molly sat in the kitchen on the other side of the door, doing her homework and wondering what Joey was doing in there. Soon Papa and Bessie came home. Papa tried to get Mama to ask Joey to come out to supper, but the most she would agree to was letting Bessie bring him a plate of food.

After supper, Bessie said, "We didn't have a concert for a long time. How about it?"

Molly knew she was doing it for Joey. He loved to sing.

"Aw, you just want to sing 'Yakke Hula,' " Molly said, playing along.

"Is the song about me?" Yaaki asked.

Everyone laughed. It did sound a little like his name. Bessie knew only the first line of her favorite song: "Yakke Hula, Hickey Doola." No one expected her to sing.

"You start, Ma," Molly said.

Mama sang her favorite song, "Play, Fiddle, Play." Joey loved hearing Mama sing it, and Molly could imagine him listening, with his ear to the door.

"It's your turn, Pa," Rebecca said.

"I'm not singing until I have a bigger audience," Papa said, nodding at Joey's door.

"Come on, Ma . . ." Molly said.

"He's sorry, Laya . . ." Bessie said.

Mama gave in. She turned to Joey's door. "Joey, Papa wants a bigger audience," she said.

Joey didn't have to be told. He could hear every word. Everyone watched the door open. Joey, his eyes red from crying, sat down with Yaaki.

"What shall I sing?" Papa asked. He had learned two songs in World War I, "The Barber Song" and "I'm a Twelve-O'clock Fella in a Ten-O'clock Town."

" 'The Barber Song,' " Molly, Joey, and Rebecca shouted, choosing the shorter song. Papa did not have a very good voice.

Papa leaned back in his chair and sang:

"Good morning, Mr. Zip Zip Zip,
good morning, Mr. Zip Zip Zip,
with your hair cut just as short,
with your hair cut just as short,
with your hair cut just as short
as mine."

Everyone clapped. Molly felt good, with Mama and
Joey talking again, and Joey right there. Everything would
have been perfect, if only Tsippi were there too.

"You go, Rebecca," Molly said. "Sing 'The Lion's
Song,'" she added quickly, naming a short song.

Rebecca stood in front of the refrigerator and sang:

"When the lions roar, they say,
'You had better keep away.
GRR RRR, keep away.'"

Everyone clapped. "That's a nice song," Yaaki said,
clapping along.

"Are you going to sing, Yaaki?" Papa asked.

"I don't know a song yet," Yaaki said, and blew his
own voice through the flute.

"You go, Molly," Rebecca said.

"Me?" Molly said. "I'm a listener. I can't carry a tune.
But I wrote a poem in school. I'll read it."

She got the sheet from her notebook and stood facing
the family.

"The name of it is 'Winter,'" she said.

"The winter is so very cold.
It chaps my hands and knees,
It makes my breath go up in smoke
And makes me—BRR!—just freeze.

"O, snow, get off the ground, I say,
It's time for summer's heat.
Begone from Borough Park, O snow,
Stop falling on my street."

She blushed with pleasure to hear the family applaud. She hadn't read the poem in class. The bell had rung before Miss Tuck could call on her.

"I want Joey to sing," Yaaki said.

"What should I sing?" Joey asked.

Everyone spoke at once. " 'When You Wish Upon a Star.' " " 'Chattanooga Choo Choo.' " " 'White Cliffs of Dover.' "

Joey looked at Mama. "What do you want to hear, Ma?"

"The song about the angels dancing," she said.

Joey knew what she meant. He sang "Anniversary Waltz." His voice was beginning to change and it cracked a little, but it was still sweet and tuneful.

Molly beamed with pride, listening. Tsippi loved to hear Joey sing too. Molly wished she were there.

CHAPTER THIRTEEN

Glad Again

The next morning, as Molly was getting ready for school, Mama stood trying to thread a needle by the light of the window and Yaaki held the bottom of the thread, helping her.

"I forgot to look," Molly said, reaching into the closet for her coat. "Did the snow stick?"

Mama glanced outside. "No, the sidewalk is clean," she said.

Rebecca was already dressed and waiting. Molly opened the door.

"We're going," she called, as she and Rebecca stepped out into the hall.

Molly hoped, as she walked along, that Tsippi would speak to her today. It seemed to her that she had done all that she could do and that Tsippi ought to forgive her by now.

"Please speak to me today, Tsippi," Molly said, sending the words out mentally. "We're even. Let's be friends again. I miss you so much."

She had the feeling when she dropped Rebecca off and went up the stairs that Tsippi had heard her today. She was so sure of it, she expected Tsippi to come running up to her as she entered class. Instead, Tsippi remained standing at the back of the room, talking to Big Naomi and Ruthie. Ruthie looked up and waved but Tsippi didn't.

Molly wondered, as she took her seat, why she kept forgetting about Ruthie.

The starting bell rang, and Miss Tuck closed the door and went to her seat.

Molly took out her homework.

"I'm sure you have all been able to find a favorite holiday to write about," Miss Tuck said with a smile. "Anyone care to be the first volunteer?"

Molly was surprised to see Beverly's hand shoot up.

"Beverly," Miss Tuck called.

Beverly went to the front with her homework and stood beside Miss Tuck reading about the Fourth of July. Molly couldn't help but feel that Beverly had copied the homework out of the encyclopedia. So as not to have to face Beverly when she returned, Molly glanced over her shoulder, hoping to catch Tsippi's eye as she did so, but Tsippi was not looking her way.

"Eyes front!" Miss Tuck said. "Raymond!" she called.

Molly looked front and listened to Raymond read about Lincoln's Birthday. He said it was his favorite holiday because Lincoln was his favorite president. Molly noticed, as he read, that his lips were bluish. She glanced around to see if any of the other boys had blue lips, and none did.

Providence got up next to read about Christmas. Again Molly tried to reach Tsippi mentally. "Please come up to me today. Let's start being friends again," she said.

Miss Tuck next called on Vinnie. Molly was glad when she heard him reading about May Procession Day. It wasn't an American holiday but a Catholic one, when children dressed up to parade around for the Virgin Mary, then went home for ice cream and cake. Molly had writ-

ten about Passover, which was a Jewish holiday. She
had planned only to hand it in. But since Vinnie had
read about a Catholic holiday, she felt free to read it
and raised her hand.

"Molly," Miss Tuck said.

Molly went to the front and stood beside the teacher's
desk. For the first time, she had a direct view of Tsippi.
Molly could not take her eyes from her friend.

"We're waiting, Molly," Miss Tuck said.

Reluctantly, Molly looked away. "It's a poem," she
said.

"Fine," Miss Tuck said.

"It's long, two stanzas," Molly said.

"If you haven't finished reading when the bell rings,
you'll just have to stop," Miss Tuck said.

Molly smiled. The poem was long, but not that long.

"Start, already!" someone called from the back.

"The name of the poem is 'Passover,'" Molly said,
and read:

"When the Jews were slaves in Egypt,
Moses set them free.
He led them to the Promised Land
That lay across the sea."

She paused after the first stanza, glanced at Miss Tuck
to see if she had the teacher's attention, then continued:

"When our relatives come to the seder,
Our kitchen table, so small,
Is stretched and stretched until
There is room to sit for all."

She didn't know if the poem was any good and felt
shy as she returned to her seat.

Molly fell to thinking about Passover as Miss Tuck spoke to the class about the importance of holidays. Tsippi had been at Molly's family's *seder* last year. Now it looked as if Tsippi wouldn't be there. The thought hurt. Molly reminded herself that her crime had been much worse than Tsippi's and resolved to try again. She felt a little hopeful. Before, when she had looked at Tsippi, Tsippi had met her glance for the first time.

Thinking about what to do, Molly decided the best time to speak to Tsippi was at the wardrobe, when they went for their coats. But later, when the noon bell rang and she went for her coat, she saw Tsippi grab hers and rush out into the hall.

Molly ran after her, trying to catch her, but Tsippi had disappeared in the crowd.

Big Naomi and Ruthie were walking by. "Hey," Big Naomi said. "How did you like Beverly going to the front of the room to read?"

Ruthie giggled. "I didn't think she could read," she said.

That was the first time Molly heard Ruthie say anything like that. She fell in with the girls, walking to the staircase.

"I thought she copied it out of the encyclopedia," Molly said.

"I thought the same thing," Ruthie said.

Downstairs, the two girls went out and Molly went around the stairs to get Rebecca. As she started for home with her, Molly realized that this would be the best time to catch Tsippi. She was at home, eating lunch. Molly crossed Rebecca at the corner and told her to go on alone. She watched, waiting to see that her sister was safely on the way, then went back up the street to Tsippi's building and rang the bell.

Like the last time, Tsippi came to the door.

Molly forced herself to speak. "I wondered if you got my letter," she said.

"I got it," Tsippi said.

"Did you read it?"

"I read it."

Molly waited, but Tsippi said nothing more.

"I'm sorry for everything," Molly said. "I was jealous of Big Naomi and I wanted to hurt you because you stopped being my best friend."

"I never stopped," Tsippi said.

"You did."

"I didn't."

Molly looked at Tsippi. "I saw you, that time I asked you to come to my house to do homework," she said.

"What about it?" Tsippi said. She seemed not to understand.

"You said you couldn't come," Molly said. "Then I saw you with Naomi, in front of her father's pushcart."

"You saw me?" Tsippi asked.

"From the bakery window. I went to get a bread for my mother."

Tsippi glanced away. "I couldn't help it," she said. "She told me she had nobody to talk to about the period. She couldn't talk to her father. I felt sorry for her. I promised to talk to her after school."

"Why didn't you tell me?" Molly said.

"I didn't want you to think—anything," Tsippi answered.

"It was like a lie," Molly said.

"It wasn't a lie."

"It was like a lie. And what about the time you told her to meet you at my house?" Molly asked, smarting under the memory of the insult.

"I didn't know about that," Tsippi said. "I didn't tell her to come. I didn't want her to. She just came."

Molly believed Tsippi. "Should we be friends again?" she asked.

Tsippi nodded.

Molly glanced over Tsippi's shoulder into the empty apartment. "You want to come to my house for lunch?" she said.

Tsippi shook her head. "I can't. My stepmother left lunch. I can't waste it."

"It's Passover soon," Molly said.

"I know."

"You coming to the *seder*?"

Tsippi nodded and reached under her glasses to wipe away a tear.

Molly was on the point of tears herself. "I better go," she said. "My mother will be wondering . . ."

Molly rushed home. She did not understand the way she felt. Usually, when she was happy, she wanted to sing her happiness song. But now, even though she was so happy, so very happy, all she wanted to do was cry.

CHAPTER FOURTEEN

Prepared

Overnight, Molly's life had changed. It was back to what it had been before, only better. She and Tsippi were friends again. The weather had turned nice, and chapped knees and lips were gone forever—at least for a while. Molly was tickled pink with the way that the week went. On Friday, not only did Tsippi come over to hear the family sing Sabbath table songs, Ruthie Riness did too. And on Sunday, when Molly and Tsippi and Ruthie went to see the new Bette Davis movie at the Windsor, Nice Beverly also went along.

On the walk back home from the movies, seeing that she had both Tsippi and Nice Beverly there, two girls who had *it*, Molly thought she would try to get more information.

"It's funny," she said, "but when I see Bette Davis, I can't believe that everyone, even movie stars, gets the period."

"Me too," Ruthie said.

"I used to be like that, before I got it," Beverly said. "But I don't think about it anymore. You get used to it."

"Not me," Tsippi said.

Molly giggled. "How could you? You only had it once."

"You can't be used to it yet," Beverly said.

Molly had brought the conversation around to where she wanted it.

"You know, Tsippi," she said, "I read that book you gave me a hundred times. I still don't understand what happens."

"Well . . ." Tsippi began.

Beverly answered for her. "You see a little stain at first, then a little more for a few days, then it's over," she said.

Molly asked more questions. She felt grown-up, and proud, to have Tsippi and Beverly speak freely before her. Soon she had a pretty good idea of the period, better than from the book. There was nothing for her to do— she did not have the period. But she could prepare herself, and be ready when it came.

That evening, after supper, Rebecca went next door to visit Mrs. Chiodo, Joey went out with his friends, and Papa went to a meeting of the Jewish War Veterans. Yaaki was out in the hall, playing with a little girl who lived upstairs. Only Mama and Bessie were at home. They were expecting Tillie and Goldie to come over. Mama had put the sponge cake on the table, and Bessie lit a fire under the kettle.

This, Molly thought, would be a good time to go to the drugstore. She took some of the allowance money she had saved in her drawer.

"Ma," she said, "I have to get something from Tsippi's house. I'll be back soon."

"Fine," Mama said. She and Bessie were hurrying to get the dishes dried and out of the way before the company came.

Molly left the house and went to the drugstore. She felt shy as she entered. She had only been there before to buy iodine, rubbing alcohol, and such things. A customer, a man, was standing at the counter, and she stood to the side, waiting for him to leave.

"Yes?" the druggist said.

Molly went to the counter and put down her money.

"Sanitary napkins," she said, looking at the ceiling.

The druggist left and soon returned with a box wrapped in white paper and tied with string. Molly couldn't bring herself to look at it. As if she were studying the insides of the drugstore, she glanced from the wall to the ceiling.

"There it is," the druggist said. "Your package."

Molly took the package, along with her change. She didn't want the druggist to know it was for her. But she wasn't sure she would know how to use it.

"It's for my mother," she said. "I wonder if she'll know how to use it."

The man stared at her. "There are instructions inside," he said.

Molly took her purchase and went home. She walked around Yaaki, playing in the hall, and opened the door slowly. Mama, Bessie, Tillie, and Goldie were sitting around the kitchen table, talking. Molly hurried through the kitchen, keeping close to the wall and holding the package between herself and the wall. No one lifted an eye.

In her room she emptied the contents of the box, and the instruction sheet, into her drawer and covered it up with socks and underwear. She flattened the box, folded it, and put it in her schoolbag, to throw it away in the school garbage can tomorrow. The paper she saved for Yaaki.

As she stood before the bureau mirror and caught sight of herself, she thought she detected a rise on her chest. She looked in the mirror again but still wasn't sure. So she could tell, she unbuttoned her blouse, pulled her undershirt tight, and looked down at her chest. She had been wrong.

Molly buttoned her blouse. She looked at herself in the mirror, wondering if she was pretty. How could she tell? She knew Bette Davis was pretty, but she couldn't tell about herself.

"A good character is more important," she told herself and shrugged. Her eye fell on the coins lying on the bureau, the change from her purchase. She went into the kitchen and put the coins in the charity box on the shelf.

Goldie looked up. "Look at that, Molly's giving money to charity," she said.

Molly smiled at her and went to the living room.

"She's a good girl," she heard Bessie say.

Bessie said that often. But Molly always liked hearing it. She was pleased with herself. She had prepared, and it made her feel good. She remembered the magazine Nice Beverly had lent her and went to get it. It was a *Street and Smith Love Story*. She had never read one before.

She sat down on the couch with the magazine. Enjoying the way she felt, enjoying having the couch to herself, the silence in the living room, the cozy voices in the kitchen, she opened the magazine and began to read.

CHAPTER FIFTEEN

Passover Comes

The day of Passover, Miss Tuck let the whole class out early. In the excitement and shuffle on the stairs, Molly became separated from Tsippi and Ruthie. Tsippi was somewhere above her and Ruthie below. Molly had no trouble locating Ruthie, on account of the straight part.

Outside, she waited in the school yard for the girls to find her, and soon both were at her side.

"Ruthie," Molly said, "I never could figure out how you get your part so straight."

"I have long hair, and it's thick," Ruthie said. She took a handful and held it up. "Here, feel it."

Molly felt it.

"Yeah, it is thick. Mine is so thin and fly-ey," she added, giving Ruthie's hair to Tsippi to feel.

"Umm," Tsippi said. She leaned over and whispered to Molly, "I have to tell you something."

Molly didn't know how to handle the situation. Tsippi didn't want to speak in front of Ruthie. But Molly didn't want Ruthie to feel left out. She began to walk slowly toward the gate, dragging her feet. Tsippi walked along at the same pace.

"You're too slow for me, I have to get home," Ruthie said, hurrying toward the gate.

"Are you coming over tomorrow?" Molly called after her.

"Uh-huh, after lunch," Ruthie called back.

Molly turned to Tsippi. "What?" she asked.

"I didn't want to say anything, in case Ruthie got jealous," Tsippi said. "But my stepmother won't let me come to your *seder* tonight."

"Why?" Molly asked, surprised.

"On account of the period. Can you believe it?" Tsippi asked.

"The period? What has that got to do with it?" Molly asked. "Besides," she added, puzzled, "didn't you just have it?"

Tsippi nodded. "It comes every month," she said. "She says on the first day it's better to stay around the house."

Molly could see that Tsippi was as disappointed as she was. She headed for the gate, with Tsippi beside her.

"I'll see you tomorrow, though," Tsippi added. "I'll be there after lunch too."

"Okay," Molly said.

The girls parted at the school-yard gate, Tsippi crossing over to her house and Molly walking on down the street to go home.

As she opened the door to the house she found the way to the kitchen blocked by the table. She had expected to see a long table. A bridge table was always added to the regular table on holidays, to make more seating space. But the table today seemed abnormally long. Molly soon saw why.

The table was lumpy in two places. Two bridge tables had been added this time, one at either end. But a white cloth covered it all and the table looked nice despite the lumps, with a stack of matzo at one end, a plate with Passover foods in the middle, and wine glasses—

wine for the grown-ups and grape juice for the children—beside each plate.

Molly stepped around the table.

Mama was at the sink, and Bessie was sucking in her breath to make herself skinny so she could walk around the table and leave a *Haggadah*, the little book that was read at the *seder*, near each plate.

"Hi," Molly said.

No one answered.

"How come the table's so long?" she asked.

Again no one answered.

She looked into the living room. Papa was in the easy chair, smoking and reading the paper. Yaaki, all dressed up for the *seder*, sat in the other chair, singing into a comb covered with toilet paper to make music. Rebecca was on the couch, coloring in the new coloring book Mrs. Chiodo had brought her last night.

Molly realized what was so peculiar about the house. It was silent. No one was speaking.

"Why is it so quiet here?" she asked.

"Can't you see I'm busy?" Mama said, stirring a pot on the stove.

"When is Mordi coming?" Molly asked, as much to break the silence as to find out.

"Soon," Mama said. "They'll all be here soon—Esther, her new husband, Mordi . . ."

"The Menites are coming too," Rebecca said.

"The Menites?" Molly asked. "Who are they?"

Papa flicked his cigarette into the metal ashtray on the arm of his chair and said nothing.

"Mama's not talking to Papa because he invited the Menites to the *seder*," Rebecca said.

"What is Rebecca talking about?" Molly said. "Who are the Menites anyhow? Do I know them?"

Mama wiped her hands on her apron. "Not Menites, Yemenites," she said. "They're dark Jews, from Yemen. Your father met the boy in the synagogue. He has no father. So your father invited him to the *seder*. And his mother. And his sister . . ."

Molly knew that whenever Mama referred to Papa as *your father,* her parents had had an argument. But she could not understand why Mama was so disturbed. "So?" she said. "What's wrong with that? The Bible says you're supposed to invite strangers to your table. You told me yourself."

Mama flung her voice into the living room. "Yes, we're supposed to, but it should be discussed first," she said.

Papa's voice came floating in. "Where is your Jewish heart?" he said.

"A Jewish heart I have," Mama answered. "But whose Jewish hands and feet were cleaning and cooking and baking all day? Yours? Or mine?"

Papa got up from his chair and came into the kitchen. "I said it once, I'll say it again. I'm sorry. Next time I'll ask you first."

Bessie stood looking from Mama to Papa. "Laya," she said, "he apologized; let it be finished."

"You're supposed to invite orphans and strangers," Molly repeated, trying to help Bessie make peace. She remembered Tsippi's disappointing news.

"Tsippi isn't coming to the *seder*," she added.

Mama glanced at her, then turned away. "A stranger will always be welcome at my table," she said.

Soon the door opened and Esther came in, followed

· 115 ·

by Julius, her new husband, and Mordi.

"Happy holiday, *gut yontiff*!" Esther called.

Rebecca and Yaaki came running in from the living room. Everyone started hugging and kissing. Molly hugged her cousin and let herself be hugged by her aunt. She looked the new uncle over as he shook hands with Papa. Mama and Papa had met him at the wedding, but Molly had never seen him before. He had curly hair and red cheeks. She had heard stories about married people and she glanced away, embarrassed.

As everyone stood huddled in the crowded kitchen, Bessie took away their coats and brought them into Joey's room.

"Molly," Mama said, "this is your uncle Julius."

The name made Molly think of Julie. "Hello," she said, unable to bring herself to look at him, gazing over his shoulder.

Bessie returned and began mussing Mordi's hair. "How do you doodle?" she said.

"F-f-fine," he answered with a smile.

Molly gave her little cousin another hug. He was as short as ever. He hadn't grown an inch. "Mordi, you look taller," she said to make him feel good.

"Naaa," he answered. "I'm still four feet two. I m-m-made a m-mark on the wall. I m-m-measure myself every day."

"Come, people," Mama said, taking Esther by the arm. "Let's go in the living room and sit down, till Joey and Mrs. Gamlieli come."

"I *thought* the table was bigger," Esther said. "Who is Mrs. Gamlieli?"

"I'll tell you later," Mama said. "Come, come," she

added, shepherding everyone into the living room. "There's no space here even for a clopespin."

"Clothespin, Ma," Molly called after her, correcting her.

Molly, Rebecca, Yaaki, and Mordi found themselves together in the crowded kitchen.

"Joey's not home," Molly said. "Let's go sit in his room."

Rebecca, Yaaki, and Mordi followed her inside. Molly shoved the coats aside to make room on the bed, and everyone jumped up and sat at one end, facing the courtyard window. They spied on the people in the opposite window, ducking behind the coats and laughing each time they were seen.

Molly played along with them, laughing and ducking at the same time. She was having fun and she wondered if Tsippi still had fun now that she was a woman. Soon Molly heard strange voices in the kitchen.

"That must be the Yemenites," she said, jumping down off the bed.

The children followed her out into the kitchen. There was hardly any room to stand, but Mama, Papa, Esther, and Julius were gathered around a small dark woman who was very fat and wore rings on her fingers and a gold chain around her neck. A boy older than Joey stood on one side of her and a teenage girl on the other.

Mama turned to Molly and the children. "This is Molly, Rebecca, and Yaaki, our children. And that's Mordi, my sister's little boy. Children," she added, "this is Mrs. Gamlieli, Eli, and Raqel."

Molly looked them over, wishing the boy and girl were closer to her own age.

Mrs. Gamlieli stood smiling down at Yaaki. "He looks like an angel," she said, speaking with an accent that Molly had never heard before.

The door opened and Joey came in.

"Good, good," Mama said. "Now everyone's here." She introduced Joey to Julius and to the Gamlieli family, then moved to the front of the table and told everyone where to sit.

Molly found herself seated across the table from Raqel and between Yaaki and Julius. She moved her chair closer to Yaaki so as not to brush up against Julius by accident.

"Where's Tsippi?" Rebecca asked.

"She couldn't come," Molly said.

"I'm sorry," Bessie said, glancing around the crowded table, "but maybe it's a good thing. Nobody else could fit, it's so crowded here."

Men were supposed to wear *yarmulkes*, skull caps, and Papa walked around to give Julius, Joey, and Eli each one.

"Give me one too," Yaaki said.

"I was coming to give you one," Papa said, putting a cap on Yaaki's head.

Molly wondered why only men wore *yarmulkes*. "Pa," she said, "why don't girls have to cover their heads too?"

"A *yarmulke* is a sign of respect to God," he said. "Men wear it to remind themselves. But women are naturally closer to God. They don't have to be reminded."

Molly nodded. The explanation satisfied her. She felt close to God. She talked to God all the time.

She caught Julius smiling at her and glanced away.

Papa next went around the table pouring wine. Molly leaned toward Yaaki so as not to come in contact with

Julius as Papa filled her glass. She saw with delight that Papa had given her half water and half wine this time, same as Joey. Her arm accidentally brushed against Julius and she drew away.

"What page do we start on, Pa?" Joey asked.

Papa opened the book. "Page three," he said. "We'll take turns reading the story of when the Israelites were slaves in Egypt, and how Moses set them free."

"We read that story last year," Rebecca said.

Molly found Raqel smiling at her and smiled back.

"That's right," Papa said. "The story is three thousand years old. We tell it every year. That's how we celebrate the holiday."

"And I g-get to ask the f-f-four questions, like last year," Mordi said.

"Right," Papa answered. "The youngest always asks the four questions about why this night is different from any other night."

"I'm the youngest," Yaaki said.

"That's true," Papa answered. "Do you know how to read?"

Yaaki shook his head.

"Next year, when you know how, you'll ask the four questions."

Across the table from Molly Joey was talking to Raqel, and Mama was listening to Mrs. Gamlieli.

"My husband died four months ago," Mrs. Gamlieli said. "He was a jeweler."

Molly looked at her rings and chain. She could believe it.

"Let's start, Papa," Rebecca said.

"Yeah, Pa," Joey said. "We can't eat until we finish

reading the story, and we haven't even started yet."

Papa turned to Mama. "Laya," he said, "they want me to begin. Do I have your permission?"

Mama looked at him. "What kind of question is that?"

"I didn't want to begin without first asking you," Papa said with a straight face.

Molly and Bessie smiled at each other.

"What do you mean, Avram?" Esther asked.

"It's a joke," Bessie said.

"Begin already," Mama said. She turned to Esther. "I'll tell you later," she added.

Papa lifted his glass of wine. "Blessed is the Eternal, our God, ruler of the universe, who created the fruit of the vine," he said, and took a sip of wine.

Molly took a sip of her watery wine. "Amen," she said, along with everyone else.

She glanced around the table and was filled with a great sense of well-being. She felt lucky to be sitting there, surrounded by relatives and friends. She wished Tsippi and Ruthie could have been there too. That would have made it perfect. But she would be seeing them to-morrow. She felt a burst of joy, and as she always did when she felt that happy, she sang her happiness song to herself behind closed lips:

> 'I should worry, I should care,
> I should marry a millionaire.''

"Molly!" Papa was saying. "We're waiting for you to catch up."

She saw that he, and everyone else, had taken a second sip of wine.

"Amen," she said, feeling good, and took another sip.